THE VOICE ABOVE THE WHISPERS

In Vienna, Antonio Salieri lives in solitude, an aging man who has outlived his years of glory. Meanwhile, in the city, the whispers go on and on.

Was it true that many years before, this man had murdered the greatest composer of the age, the immortal Mozart?

Only Salieri could answer this question. And on the last night of his life, he reveals the full, shocking, haunting story of—

AMADEUS

"A powerful play that examines the creative personality and the ironies that reassure us that Fate has a well-tuned humor."

—*Library Journal*

"*Amadeus* may be a play inspired by music and death, but it fills the theater with that moving, heavenly silence that is the overwhelming terror of life."

—*The New York Times*

PETER SHAFFER'S previous theatrical triumphs include *Equus*, which ran for over a thousand performances on Broadway and won the Tony Award and the Drama Critic's Award; *Five Finger Exercise*, another Drama Critic Award winner; *The Private Ear and the Public Eye; The Royal Hunt of the Sun;* and *Black Comedy*.

𝒞   𝒮

Outstanding Contemporary Plays in SIGNET CLASSIC and SIGNET Editions

(0451)

☐ **TWO PLAYS BY BERTOLT BRECHT: The Good Woman of Setzuan and The Caucasian Chalk Circle. Revised English versions and Introduction by Eric Bentley.** Foreword by Richard Gilman. This volume, by one of the towering figures of twentieth-century theater, represent Brecht at his most brilliant. Both point out with telling accuracy the very real imperfections of our social order and the dilemmas of our human condition. (517180—$4.95)*

☐ **WHO'S AFRAID OF VIRGINIA WOOLF? by Edward Albee.** The stunning play that has become a classic in our time. "A brilliantly original work of art—an excoriating theatrical experience, surging with shocks of recognition and dramatic fire."—*Newsweek*
(121252—$3.50)*

☐ **THE AMERICAN DREAM and THE ZOO STORY by Edward Albee.** Two more critically acclaimed plays by the major American playwright, author of *Who's Afraid of Virginia Woolf?*
(122933—$2.50)

☐ **THE SANDBOX and THE DEATH OF BESSIE SMITH by Edward Albee.** Two explosive off-Broadway hits, one about a scathing domestic tragedy, the other baring the ugly circumstances surrounding the death of a great Black blues singer. (112954—$2.50)

☐ **LUTHER by John Osborne.** A brilliant play about the rebellious priest who challenged and changed the spiritual world of his time, by the author of *Look Back in Anger.* (127870—$2.95)†

*Prices slightly higher in Canada
†Not available in Canada

Peter Shaffer's

AMADEUS

*With a New Introduction to
the Film Edition by the Author*

A SIGNET BOOK
NEW AMERICAN LIBRARY

For
ROBERT
with love

PREFACE

Amadeus opened at the National Theatre of Great Britain in November 1979. According to Peter Hall, the director of the play and of the theatre, it constituted the single greatest success enjoyed by this celebrated institution since its founding. At the moment of writing, one year after its premiere, the *Sunday Times* of London reports that audiences begin lining up at six o'clock in the morning to buy the few tickets which are sold only on the day of performance. This is hardly a usual practice with the Great British Public.

I mention these agreeable facts only so that I may be believed when I assert that it is not because the play was a failure in England that I made changes when it came to be produced in America. On the contrary, it is entirely the exciting success of the piece which has emboldened me to try to improve it.

The entire run of *Amadeus* in Washington, where the play was presented prior to its appearance at the Broadhurst Theatre in New York, was characterized by the most intense work. I have never before altered material in a play so extensively. I was led on to do this by what became a nearly obsessive pursuit of clarity, structural order, and drama. I was supported in these endeavors by the most understanding of directors, as well as by the most enthusiastic company of actors and the most patient stage management. I would like to thank them all deeply for their unflagging help—without which, truly, this work could not possibly have been achieved.

One of the faults which I believe existed in the London version was simply that Salieri had too little to do with Mozart's ruin. In the second act he was too often reduced to prowling hungrily around the outside of the composer's apartment, watching his decline without sufficiently contributing to it. Dramatically speaking, Salieri seemed to me to be too much the observer of the calamities he should have been causing. Now, in this new version, he seems to me to stand where he properly belongs—at the wicked center of the action.

This new, more active Salieri offers himself as a substitute father when Leopold Mozart dies. He establishes a much closer human contact with Wolfgang. And he finally induces the trusting composer to betray the rituals of the Freemasons in *The Magic Flute*. I have of course taken certain liberties with this part of the story. I have no reason to believe that the Masons actually repudiated Mozart, or that Baron Van Swieten announced that he would never speak to him again. Nevertheless, Masonic anger over *The Magic Flute* constitutes one of the most persistent rumors attached to the Mozartian legend; and the worthy Baron actually did pay for a third-class funeral when he could have easily afforded much better, for the composer he had patronized, which does suggest some deep offense which Mozart had given him. Indeed, one totally absurd story, which never quite dies out, actually implicates the Masons in causing Mozart's early death!

The great gain in dramatic terms is that I can now show the (factually true) visit of Salieri and his mistress to a performance of *The Magic Flute*. I must confess to a fondness for this new scene. It is rowdy and vigorous; it contains devices of mime which are pleasingly theatrical; it dramatizes the moment—previously only hinted at—when Salieri perceives Mozart to be himself the flute of God; and it enables me to transform the huge accusing silhouette of Leopold-as-Commendatore, seen on the backdrop, into the forgiving silhouette of Leopold-as-Sarastro, his hands extended to the world in a vast embrace of love. This transformation immeasurably clarifies the mental journey which Mozart made from *Don Giovanni* to *The Magic Flute.*

I regret that pressure of dramatic time has forced me to omit totally the theme of Aloysia, Constanze's sister, to whom Mozart was initially engaged. She was referred to frequently in the London production, and formed the subject of another transformation. Salieri was able to point out that in depicting the two seduced sisters in *Così Fan Tutte,* Mozart had clearly immortalized the Weber girls. Regretfully I had to leave out all verbal references to *Così* if I was to include those concerning *The Magic Flute:* there were otherwise simply too many descriptions of operas in the play.

The main change in *Amadeus,* however, is concerned with the treatment of the Masked Figure who came to Mozart to commission a Requiem Mass, and whom Mozart in the frenzy of his sick imagination came to regard as the Messenger of Death.

In London this Figure was actually Salieri's

grim servant Greybig, a religious fanatic dispatched by his murderous master to drive Mozart toward madness. My dissatisfaction with this theatrical idea lay mainly in my awareness that Salieri could not possibly guess that Mozart would react to the appearance of the Figure in the demented way we know he did. This was to read history backwards. And anyway, such tactics did not consort at all with the character of my oblique and indirect villain. My unease ended in the total removal of Greybig from the play, since he had no other real function than to be this Messenger of Death.

There ensued what was for me a tense period in Washington, after we had already opened the play, when I experimented with a series of new confrontation scenes between Salieri and Mozart, dispensing with a masked figure altogether. Ian McKellen and Tim Curry—the actors chiefly concerned—were heroic in assisting me—putting in, playing, and taking out several versions of this climactic passage. Their patience and dedication finally enabled me to discover what I wanted. The play now boasts a much better scene on a human level than the one we played in London. I even finally replaced the mask on Salieri's face: but by this time he was not a crudely melodramatic figure —a spooky, improbable Messenger of Death— but a more poetic and dangerous apparition, a

Messenger from God stepping out of Mozart's confessed dreams. This scene was composed with the active and generous encouragement of Peter Hall, who displayed throughout this period of trial a most miraculous calm, and who staged the final result with superb assurance. The unmasking of Salieri by Mozart from behind, for example, is a wonderful gestural climax which relieved the scene of any coarseness. No praise can be too high for Hall's creative skill under pressure.

Finally I would like to express my deepest gratitude to Michael Bessie, my dear and excellent publisher, for the saintly restraint which he has displayed during the long process of work which has produced this final version of *Amadeus*.

PETER SHAFFER

INTRODUCTION TO THE FILM EDITION

The cinema is a worrying medium for the stage playwright to work in. Its unverbal essence offers difficulties to anyone living largely by the spoken word. Increasingly, as American films grow ever more popular around the world, it is apparent that the most successful are being spoken in "Screenspeak," a kind of cinematic Esperanto equally comprehensible in Bogota and Bulawayo. For example, dialogue in heavy-action pictures, horrific or intergalactic, now consists almost entirely of the alternation of two single words—a cry and a whisper—needing translation nowhere on the planet: *"Lessgidowdaheer!"* and *"Omygaad!"* Mastery of this new tongue is not easy for older writers.

Equally dismaying has to be the endemic restlessness of film-goers. In his mind's ear, as he writes for the live theater, the dramatist can presume the attentiveness of his audience: its mutual agreement to listen and to remain in one place while the performance is going on. No such agreement exists among movie audiences. Indeed, the very word "movies" nowadays can as accurately describe the viewers of films as films themselves. I never really understood the meaning of the phrase "upward mobility" until I had experienced a Manhattan cinema on a recent Saturday night.

All of which is by way of saying that but for the enthusiasm of Mr. Milos Forman I doubt if there would be a film of *Amadeus* at all. He met me in London after the very first preview of the play at the National Theatre in November, 1979, and declared without hesitation that what I had actually written was a natural film, and that if I were ever willing to let him do so, he would direct it. In this assertion he persisted for two years.

Persistence was coupled with perceptiveness. When finally I cautiously agreed to explore the possibility of working with him, he sensed quite plainly my unease about films in general, and my dissatisfaction with all previous films of my own plays in particular. When I asked him what he would do with my piece, he told me what he would *not* do: turn it into a stagy hybrid, neither play nor picture. He also pointed out that the film of a play is really a new work, another fulfillment of the same impulse that had created the original. The adapter's task was to explore many new paths in order to emerge in the end at the same emotional place. During this process a fair amount of demolition work would go on, some of it perhaps painful to the author. In the case of *Amadeus*, its operatic stylization would probably have to go, and its language would have to be made less formal, though not automatically more juvenile.

Actually my own personal taste in cinema inclines very much to the operatic and stylized— the opening sequence of *The Magnificent Ambersons*, for example, or the iconographic groupings in the first part of *Ivan the Terrible*—but I also sensed, as we talked, how this vigorous man's brand of naturalism, infused with his huge humor and his obvious passion for my material, might make an enthralling new thing out of it. The possibility of working with him was suddenly tempting.

Certainly I was not afraid of new approaches. In composing the play I had spent over a year simply finding a way of beginning it. I don't know how many bewigged phantoms I had chased down how many suddenly blocked avenues before settling on the final formulation.

Why not join a brilliantly talented film director in even further exploration? Of course, partnership would mean permitting him to write the script with me, alone in his house—the Forman method, and one not easy for an author to countenance—but I reckoned that I had ultimately far more to learn than to lose from such an adventure, and finally I agreed. On the first day of February, 1982, our collaboration began.

It was a startling experience for me. In the end we spent well over four months together in a Connecticut farmhouse—five days a week, twelve hours a day—seeing virtually no other company. These were four months of sustained work, punctuated by innumerable tussles, falterings, and depressions, but also by sudden gleeful breakthroughs to relieve the monotony of the prevalent uncertainty. In some ways we made an Odd Couple, yoked together in a temporary form of marriage, cooking for each other in the evenings, and each day exploring whatever might contribute a variation on the vast theme of Mozart and Salieri. We acted out countless versions of each scene, improvising them aloud. I sat at a long refectory table extracting, writing down, and polishing all dialogue. In the process I filled at least twenty thick notebooks. Some of the talk is inevitably simpler in the film than in the play, but none of it, I hope, is Screenspeak. At my urging, Mr. Forman set out to investigate an unfamiliar world of music; at his, Mr. Shaffer set out to investigate an equally unfamiliar one of screen technique. If nothing else were to come out of this frenzied seclusion, we each discovered a new discipline and a new friendship.

From the start we agreed upon one thing: we were not making an objective "Life of Wolfgang Mozart." This cannot be stressed too strongly. Obviously, Amadeus on stage was never intended to be a documentary biography of the composer, and the film is even less of ne. Certainly we have incorporated many real elements, new as well as true. The film shows the acerbic relationship between the fretful young genius and his haughty employer, Archbishop Colloredo of Salzburg; the disastrous visit of Papa Leopold to his married son in Vienna; Wolfgang's playing of his piano concerti in the open air; his delight in dancing and billiards. But we are also blatantly claiming the grand license of the storyteller to embellish his tale with fictional ornament, and—above all—to supply it with a climax whose sole justification need be that it enthralls his audience and emblazons his theme. I believe that we have created just such a climax for the film of Amadeus.

To me there is something pure about Salieri's pursuit of an eternal Absolute through music, just as there is something irredeemably impure about his simultaneous pursuit of eternal fame.

The yoking of these two clearly opposed drives led us finally to devise a climax totally different from that of the play: a nightlong encounter between the physically dying Mozart and the spiritually ravenous Salieri, motivated entirely by the latter's crazed lust to snatch a piece of divinity for himself. Quite obviously, such a scene never took place in fact. However, our concern at this point was not with fact, but with the undeniable laws of drama. It is where—holding fast to the thread of our protagonist's mania—we were finally led.

Some people may find this new climax hard to accept. Others may rejoice in it as a horribly logical end to the legend. To me it seems the most appropriate finish to our black fantasia. Even on stage I had to create a final confrontation quite outside historical record. I had to recognize and honor the change of atmosphere from clear Enlightenment to murky Gothic which inevitably occurred once the figure of the Masked Messenger was introduced. In the film this recognition is more carefully prepared for. Indeed, the motif of masked people goes all through the picture—paralleling to some extent Mozart's own preoccupation with them. After all, the three great Da Ponte operas (*The Marriage of Figaro, Don Giovanni,* and *Così fan tutte*) are all concerned with the dramatic effects of wearing disguise.

What pleased me best about this resolution

is that we were able to construct a scene that is highly effective in cinematic terms, yet wholly concerned with the least visual of all possible subjects: *music itself*. I do not believe that a stage version of this scene would have been half as effective.

Filming *Amadeus* for six months in Czechoslovakia was a testing but perhaps indispensable experience, considering our subject. Prague offers the most complete baroque and rococo setting in Europe, largely untouched by the savageries of war or city planners. It is possible to turn a camera there in a complete circle and see in its frame nothing built after Mozart's death. Architecturally, Czech buildings provide a perfect background for the story, just as aesthetically Czech faces provide a perfect foreground. The people of Central Europe are not embarrassed by wearing period costume: the smallest bit player on a day's leave from the factory looks absolutely natural in peruke and pelisse. Contemplating the audiences of extras assembled in the Tyl Theatre to watch the Mozart operas being played—the very theater where *Don Giovanni* was first produced!—one experiences the miraculous feeling of time being reclaimed from oblivion. I hope profoundly that this eerie and exquisite sensation will seep through the print on to the screen.

What I hope will not seep through is any

sense of the difficulties experienced in making the picture. These, of course, were considerable. Inevitably the very act of shooting a two-and-a-half-hour costume film entirely behind the Iron Curtain became something of an ordeal for all concerned. I keep meeting people who imagine that the business of setting up cameras and turning them on sets and actors is somehow a romantic and liberating occupation. It is impossible to convince them that the daily activity of a camera crew is just about as liberating as that of Sisyphus. On each visit I grew more and more impressed by the sheer staying power of everyone concerned: by the manner in which a hundred differing skills were kept keen and shining in the face of all that could blunt and rust them. Throughout what seemed an interminable time (for the river of Time unquestionably flows slower through the channels of Czechoslovakia than it does elsewhere), the producer, Saul Zaentz, defied all known rules laid down for the behavior of movie producers by presenting each morning to the world of delay and confusion a countenance of unalterable equanimity.

I am extremely grateful to him for this example of poise, as I am to the entire team for its endurance, and to Milos Forman, above all, for showing me how you can hold every detail of a long film in your head, simultaneously, for six frenzied months—provided that you have prepared it properly first over another six. Fine directors do not appear by accident, nor do fine pictures.

Nevertheless, despite this and all his other dazzling demonstrations to me, which may yet result one day in my attempting an original film script, our joint movie is definitely the first and last of the metamorphoses of *Amadeus*. Unlike *Equus*, it will not also become a ballet; unlike *The Royal Hunt of the Sun*, it will not become an opera. Above all, and no matter how fortunate our effort may prove in its reception, it will spawn no sequels. There will be no television series of half-hour dramas in which Salieri plots a different method of murdering Mozart each week, only to be frustrated by the wily little genius in the twenty-ninth minute. Even Mr. Forman will agree that there can be a limit to adaptation.

September, 1983   *Peter Shaffer*

ACKNOWLEDGMENTS

Throughout my writing life I have been fortunate to work with distinguished directors.

John Gielgud realized my first play, *Five Finger Exercise*, with admirable smoothness. Peter Wood achieved my double bill, *The Private Ear* and *The Public Eye*, with tremendous flair. John Dexter, with unwavering courage, conjured in turn the golden splendors of *The Royal Hunt of the Sun*, the controlled hysteria of *Black Comedy*, and the compulsive sexual anguish of *Equus*. To him I shall always be indebted for helping me discover the grammar of a bolder kind of theater.

In 1970 Peter Hall directed my play *The Battle of Shrivings* with elegance and expertise.

Nine years later he invested this present piece
with an equal authority—and added for good
measure a dazzling panache entirely appropriate to its Rococo age and subject. Before rehearsals began he promised that he would present
me with an opera; and that is precisely what he
did. The result was wholly satisfying: indeed
the genre of Amadeus might best be described
as "black opera." It is his prodigiously beautiful production which I wish to recall here.

Many of my plays have been intentionally
gestural and spectacular in effect. It has always
seemed to be impossible, therefore, to publish
their texts without any reference to their first
productions. I was deeply involved in those
productions, and attended almost all rehearsals
of them: but of course their physical realization
was largely the work of the director concerned.
For this reason I have always sought his permission before setting down minute descriptions
of stage actions in print, and this has always
been granted with ready grace. It is so granted
in the present instance and, as before, I am
most grateful for it. I would like to stress,
however, that it is no part of my desire to
imprison the play in one particular presentation;
still less to encourage the automatic borrowing
of an original director's ideas by future inter-
preters. I hope that Amadeus will enjoy a vigorous life in many differing productions.

While making my acknowledgments I wish to praise the work of John Bury and Harrison Birtwistle. Mr. Bury is a truly remarkable designer whose set of the play was so entirely beguiling that I requested—and again was kindly granted—his permission to describe it in these pages. My account of it will inevitably be inadequate, since it is finally impossible to recreate great theatrical designs in words. For this I ask his indulgence. Mr. Birtwistle is a distinguished composer in his own right, who brilliantly solved the problem of how Mozart's music should sound as heard by Salieri. It was never cheaply distorted by modern devices, yet its subtle "treatment" suggested the sublime work of a genius being experienced by another musician's increasingly agonized mind. At crucial points—the explosion of the C Minor Mass at the end of Act One, or the trombones winding eerily during the entrance of the disguised First Kapellmeister in Act Two—it was splendidly theatrical.

To Peter Hall, whose immense talent made the play gleam and glitter in the world, I can only offer the extreme of my gratitude.

THE SET

Amadeus can and should be played in a variety of settings. What is described in this text is to a large extent based on the exquisite formulation found for the play by the designer John Bury, helped into being by the director, Peter Hall. I was of course in enthusiastic agreement with this formulation, and set it down here as a tribute to exquisite work.

The set consisted basically of a handsome rectangle of patterned wood—its longest sides leading away from the viewer—set into a stage of ice-blue plastic. This surface shifted beguilingly under various lights played upon it, to show a bluish gray, or azure, or emerald green, and reflected the actors standing upon it. The entire design was undeniably modern, yet it suggested without self-consciousness the age of the Rococo. Costumes and objects were sumptuously of the period—and should always be so wherever the play is produced.

The rectangle largely represented interiors: especially those of Salieri's salon, Mozart's last apartment, assorted reception rooms and opera houses. At the back stood a grand proscenium sporting gilded cherubs blowing huge trumpets, and supporting grand curtains of sky-blue, which could rise and part to reveal an enclosed space almost the width of the area downstage. Into this space superb backdrops were flown, and superb projections thrown, to show the scarlet boxes of theaters, the trees of the Prater, or a huge gilded object composed of Masonic emblems. In it the audience could see an eighteenth-century street at night (cunningly enlarged from the lid of Mozart's own curious snuff-box) or a vast wall of gold mirrors with an immense golden fireplace, representing the encrusted Palace of Schönbrunn. In it also appeared silhouettes of scandal-mongering citizens of Vienna, or the formal figures of the Emperor Joseph II of Austria and his brocaded courtiers. This wonderful upstage space, which was in effect an immense Rococo peep show, will be referred to throughout this text as the Light Box.

* * *

On stage, before the lights are lowered in the theater, four objects are to be seen by the audience. To the left, on the wooden rectangle, stands a small table, bearing a cake-stand full of confections. In the center, farther upstage and also on the wood, stands a wheelchair of the eighteenth century, with its back to us. To the right, on the reflecting plastic, stands a beautiful fortepiano in a marquetry case. Above the stage is suspended a large chandelier showing many globes of opaque glass.

All directions will be given from the viewpoint of the audience.

Changes of time and place are indicated throughout by changes of light. In reading the text it must be remembered that the action is wholly continuous. Its fluidity is ensured by the use of servants played by actors in eighteenth-century livery, whose role it is to move the furniture and carry on props with ease and correctness while the action proceeds around them. Through a pleasant paradox of theater their constant coming and going, bearing tables, chairs or cloaks, should render them virtually invisible and certainly unremarkable. This will aid the play to be acted throughout in its proper manner: with the sprung line, gracefulness and energy for which Mozart is so especially celebrated.

CHARACTERS

ANTONIO SALIERI

WOLFGANG AMADEUS MOZART

CONSTANZE WEBER, *wife to Mozart*

JOSEPH II, *Emperor of Austria*

COUNT JOHANN KILIAN VON STRACK, *Groom of the Imperial Chamber*

COUNT FRANZ ORSINI-ROSENBERG, *Director of the Imperial Opera*

BARON GOTTFRIED VAN SWIETEN, *Prefect of the Imperial Library*

TWO "VENTICELLI"—*"Little Winds," purveyors of information, gossip and rumor*

A MAJORDOMO

SALIERI'S VALET (Silent part)

SALIERI'S COOK (Silent part)

KAPELLMEISTER BONNO (Silent part)
TERESA SALIERI, *wife of Salieri* (Silent part)
KATHERINA CAVALIERI, *Salieri's pupil* (Silent part)
CITIZENS OF VIENNA
The VENTICELLI also play the TWO GALLANTS at the party in Act One.
The CITIZENS OF VIENNA also play the SERVANTS, who move furniture and bring on props as required.

The action of the play takes place in Vienna in November 1823, and in recall, the decade 1781–1791.

AMADEUS

ACT ONE

SCENE 1

Vienna

[Darkness.
Savage whispers fill the theater. We can distinguish nothing at first from this snake-like hissing save the word Salieri! repeated here, there and everywhere around the theater. Also, the barely distinguishable word Assassin!

The whispers overlap and increase in volume, slashing the air with wicked intensity. Then the light grows Upstage to reveal the silhouettes of men and women dressed in the top hats and skirts of the early nineteenth century—CITIZENS OF VI-

ENNA, *all crowded together in the Light
Box, and uttering their scandal.*]

WHISPERERS: Salieri! . . . Salieri! . . . Salieri!

[*Upstage, in a wheelchair, with his back to
us, sits an old man. We can just see, as the
light grows a little brighter, the top of his
head, encased in an old red cap, and perhaps the shawl wrapped around his shoul-
ders.*]

Salieri! . . . Salieri! . . . Salieri!

[*Two middle-aged gentlemen hurry in from
either side, also wearing the long cloaks
and tall hats of the period. These are the
two* VENTICELLI: *purveyors of fact, rumor
and gossip throughout the play. They speak
rapidly—in this first appearance extremely
rapidly—so that the scene has the air of a
fast and dreadful overture. Sometimes they
speak to each other, sometimes to us—but
always with the urgency of men who have
ever been first with the news.*]

VENTICELLO 1: I don't believe it.

VENTICELLO 2: I don't believe it.

V.1: I don't believe it.

V.2: I don't believe it.

WHISPERERS: *Salieri!*

V.1: They say.

V.2: I hear.

V.1: I hear.

2

V.2: They say.
V.1 & V.2: *I don't believe it!*
WHISPERERS: *Salieri!*

V.1: The whole city is talking.
V.2: You hear it all over.
V.1: The cafés.
V.2: The Opera.
V.1: The Prater.
V.2: The gutter.
V.1: They say even Metternich repeats it.
V.2: They say even Beethoven, his old pupil.
V.1: But why now?
V.2: After so long?
V.1: Thirty-two years!
V.1 & V.2: *I don't believe it!*
WHISPERERS: SALIERI!

V.1: They say he shouts it out all day!
V.2: I hear he cries it out all night!
V.1: Stays in his apartments.
V.2: Never goes out.
V.1: Not for a year now.
V.2: Longer. Longer.
V.1: Must be seventy.
V.2: Older. Older.
V.1: Antonio Salieri—
V.2: The famous musician—
V.1: Shouting it aloud!
V.2: Crying it aloud!

3

V.1: Impossible.
V.2: Incredible.
V.1: I don't believe it!
V.2: I don't believe it!
WHISPERERS: SALIERI!

V.1: I know who *started* the tale!
V.2: *I* know who started the tale!
[*Two old men—one thin and dry, one very fat—detach themselves from the crowd at the back and walk down-stage, on either side: Salieri's* VALET *and* PASTRY COOK.]
V.1: [*Indicating him*]. The old man's valet!
V.2: [*Indicating him*]. The old man's cook!
V.1: The valet hears him shouting!
V.2: The cook hears him crying!
V.1: What a story!
V.2: What a scandal!
[*The* VENTICELLI *move quickly upstage, one on either side, and each collects a silent informant.* VENTICELLO ONE *walks down eagerly with the* VALET; VENTICELLO TWO *walks down eagerly with the* COOK.]
V.1: [*To* VALET]. What does he say, your master?
V.2: [*To* COOK]. What exactly does he say, the Kapellmeister?
V.1: Alone in his house—
V.2: All day and all night—
V.1: What sins does he shout?
V.2: The old fellow—

4

V.1: The recluse—

V.2: What horrors have you heard?

V.1 & V.2: *Tell us! Tell us! Tell us at once! What does he cry? What does he cry? What does he cry?*

[VALET *and* COOK *gesture toward* SALIERI.]

SALIERI: (In a great cry). MOZART!!!

[Silence]

V.1: [*Whispering*]. Mozart!

V.2: [*Whispering*]. Mozart!

SALIERI: *Perdonami, Mozart! Il tuo assassino ti chiede perdono!*

V.1: [*In disbelief*]. Pardon, Mozart!

V.2: [*In disbelief*]. Pardon your assassin!

V.1 & V.2: *God preserve us!*

SALIERI: *Pietà, Mozart! . . . Mozart, pietà!*

V.1: Mercy, Mozart!

V.2: Mozart, have mercy!

V.1: He speaks in Italian when excited!

V.2: German when not!

V.1: *Perdonami, Mozart!*

V.2: Pardon your assassin!

[*The* VALET *and the* COOK *walk to either side of the stage and stand still. Pause. The* VENTICELLI *cross themselves, deeply shocked.*]

V.1: There was talk once before, you know.

V.2: Thirty-two years ago.

V.1: When Mozart was dying.

V.2: He claimed he'd been poisoned!

V.1: Some said he accused a man.

V.2: Some said that man was Salieri!

V.1: But no one believed it.

V.2: They knew what he died of!

V.1: Syphilis, surely.

V.2: Like everybody else.

[Pause]

V.1: [Slyly]. But what if Mozart was right?

V.2: If he really was murdered?

V.1: And by him. Our First Kapellmeister!

V.2: Antonio Salieri!

V.1: It can't possibly be true.

V.2: It's not actually credible.

V.1: Because why?

V.2: Because why?

V.1 & V.2: Why on earth would he do it?

V.1: And why confess now?

V.2: After thirty-two years!

WHISPERERS: Salieri!

[Pause]

SALIERI: Mozart! Mozart! Perdonami! . . . Il tuo assassino ti chiede perdono!

[Pause. They look at him, then at each other.]

V.1: What do you think?

V.2: What do you think?

V.1: I don't believe it!

V.2: I don't believe it!

[Pause]

V.1: All the same . . .

V.2: Is it just possible?

V.1 & V.2: [Whispering]. *Did he do it after all?!*

WHISPERERS: SALIERI!

[The VENTICELLI *go off. The* VALET *and the* COOK *remain, on either side of the stage.* SALIERI *swivels his wheelchair around and stares at us. We see a man of seventy in an old stained dressing gown. He rises and squints at the audience, as if trying to see it.*]

SCENE 2

Salieri's Apartment
November 1823. The small hours

SALIERI: [*Calling to audience*]. Vi saluto! Ombri del Futuro! Antonio Salieri—a vostro servizio! [*A clock outside in the street strikes three.*] I can almost see you in your ranks—waiting for your turn to live. Ghosts of the Future! Be visible. I beg you. Be visible. Come to this dusty old room—this time, the smallest hours of dark November, eighteen hundred and twenty-three—and be my confessors! Will you not enter this place and stay with me till dawn? Just till dawn—smeary six o'clock!

WHISPERERS: *Salieri! . . . Salieri! . . .*

[*The curtains slowly descend on the* CITIZENS OF VIENNA. *Faint images of long windows are projected on the silk.*]

SALIERI: Can you hear them? Vienna is a City of Slander. Everyone tells tales here: even my servants. I keep only two now. [*He indicates them.*] They've been with me ever since I came here, fifty years ago. The keeper of the razor; the maker of the cakes. One keeps me tidy, the other keeps me full. [*To them*] "Leave me, both of you! Tonight I do not go to bed at all!"

[*They react in surprise.*]

"Return here tomorrow morning at six precisely—to shave, to feed your capricious master!" [*He smiles at them both and claps his hands in dismissal.*] Via. Via, via, via! Grazie!

[*They bow, bewildered, and leave the stage. He peers hard at the audience, trying to see it.*]

Now, won't you appear? I need you—desperately! This is the last hour of my life. Those about to die implore you! . . . What must I do to make you visible? Raise you up in the

flesh to be my last, last audience? . . . Does it
take an Invocation? That's how it's always
done in opera! Ah yes, of course: that's it. An
Invocation. The only way. [*He rises.*] Let me
try to conjure you *now*—Ghosts of the distant
Future—so I can see you.

[*He gets out of the wheelchair and huddles
over to the fortepiano. He stands at the
instrument and begins to sing in a high
cracked voice, interrupting himself at the
end of each sentence with figurations on
the keyboard in the manner of a recitativo
secco. During this, the houselights slowly
come up to illuminate the audience.*]

[*Singing*]

Ghosts of the Future!

Shades of time to come!

So much more unavoidable than those of
time gone by!

Appear with what sympathy incarnation may
endow you!

Appear you:

The yet to be born!

The yet to hate!

The yet to *kill!*

Appear . . . posterity!

[*The light on the audience reaches its
maximum. It stays like this during all of
the following.*]

[*Speaking again*] There. It worked. I can see

you! That is the result of proper training. I
was taught invocation by Gluck, who was
a true master at it. He had to be. In his day,
that was what people went to the opera for:
the raising of gods, and ghosts. Nowadays,
since Rossini became the rage, they prefer to
watch the escapades of hairdressers. [*Pause*]
Scusate. Invocation is an exhausting business!
I need refreshment. [*He sits again in his
wheelchair, moves himself over to the cake-
stand, selects a cake and eats it.*] It's a little
repellent, I admit, but actually, the first sin I
have to confess to you is gluttony. Sticky
gluttony at that. Infantine, *Italian* gluttony!
The truth is that all my life I have never been
able to conquer a lust for the sweetmeats of
Northern Italy, where I was born. From the
ages of three to seventy-three, my entire career has been conducted to the taste of al-
monds sprinkled with sifted sugar. [*Lustfully*]
Veronese biscuits! Milanese macaroons! Snow
dumplings with pistachio sauce! . . . Do not
judge me too harshly for this. All men harbor
patriotic feelings of some kind. . . . My parents were provincial subjects of the Austrian
Empire. A Lombardy merchant and his Lombardy wife. Their notion of place was the
tiny town of Legnago—which I could not
wait to leave. Their notion of God was a
superior Habsburg emperor, inhabiting a

Heaven only slightly farther off than Vienna. All they required of Him was to protect commerce, and keep them forever preserved in mediocrity. My own requirements were very different. [*Pause*] I wanted *Fame*. Not to deceive you, I wanted to blaze like a comet across the firmament of Europe! Yet only in one special way. Music! Absolute music! . . . A note of music is either right or wrong *absolutely!* Not even time can alter that: music is God's art. [*Excited by the recollection*] Already when I was ten a spray of sounded notes would make me dizzy almost to falling! By twelve, I was stumbling about under the poplar trees humming my arias and anthems to the Lord. My one desire was to join all the composers who had celebrated His glory through the long Italian past! . . . Every Sunday I saw Him in church, painted on the flaking wall. I don't mean Christ. The Christs of Lombardy are simpering sillies, with lambkins on their sleeves. No: I mean an old candle-smoked God in a mulberry robe, staring at the world with dealer's eyes. Tradesmen had put him up there. Those eyes made bargains, real and irreversible. "You gave me so—I'll give you so! No more. No less!" [*He eats a sweet biscuit in his excitement.*] The night before I left Legnago forever, I went to see Him, and made a bargain with Him myself!

I was a sober sixteen, filled with a desperate sense of right. I knelt before the God of Bargains, and I prayed through the moldering plaster with all my soul.

[*He kneels.*]

"Signore, let me be a composer! Grant me sufficient fame to enjoy it. In return, I will live with virtue. I will strive to better the lot of my fellows. And I will honor You with much music all the days of my life!" As I said Amen, I saw His eyes flare. [*As "God"*] "Bene. Go forth, Antonio. Serve Me and mankind, and you will be blessed!" . . . "*Grazie!*" I called back. "I am Your servant for life!"

[*He gets to his feet again.*]

The very next day, a family friend suddenly appeared—out of the blue—took me off to Vienna and paid for me to study music! Shortly afterwards I met the Emperor, who favored me. Clearly my bargain had been accepted!

[*Pause*]

The same year I left Lombardy, a young prodigy was touring Europe. A miraculous virtuoso aged ten years. Wolfgang Amadeus Mozart.

[*Pause. He smiles at the audience.*]

And now, gracious ladies! obliging gentlemen! I present to you—for one performance only—my last composition, entitled *The Death of*

Mozart; or, Did I Do It? ... Dedicated to posterity on this, the last night of my life!

[He bows deeply, undoing as he does so the buttons of his old dressing gown. When he straightens himself, divesting himself of this drab outer garment and his cap, he is a young man in the prime of life, wearing a sky-blue coat and the elegant decent clothes of a successful composer of the 1780s. The house lights go down again on the audience.]

SCENE 3

Transformation to the Eighteenth Century

[Music sounds softly in the background: a serene piece for strings by Salieri. SERVANTS enter. One takes away the dressing gown and cap; another places on the table a wigstand bearing a powdered wig; a third brings on a chair and places it at the left, upstage.

At the back, the blue curtains rise and part to show the EMPEROR JOSEPH II *and his* COURT *bathed in golden light, against a golden background of mirrors and an immense golden fireplace. His Majesty is seated, holding a rolled paper, listening to the music. Also listening are* COUNT VON STRACK; COUNT ORSINI-ROSENBERG; BARON VAN SWIETEN; *and an anonymous* PRIEST, *dressed in a soutane. An old wigged* COURTIER *enters and takes his place at the keyboard:* KAPELLMEISTER BONNO. SALIERI *takes his wig from the stand.*]

SALIERI: [*In a young man's voice; vigorous and confident*]. The place throughout is Vienna. The year—to begin with—1781. The age still that of the Enlightenment: that clear time before the guillotine fell in France and cut all our lives in half. I am thirty-one. Already a prolific composer to the Habsburg court. I own a respectable house and a respectable wife—Teresa.

[*Enter* TERESA: *a padded, placid lady who seats herself uprightly in the upstage chair.*] I do not mock her, I assure you. I required only one quality in a domestic companion—lack of fire. And in that omission Teresa was conspicuous. [*Ceremoniously, he puts on his powdered wig.*] I also had a prize pupil: Katherina Cavalieri.

[KATHERINA *swirls on from the opposite side: a beautiful girl of twenty. The music becomes vocal: faintly, we hear a* SOPRANO *singing a* CONCERT *aria. Like* TERESA's, KATHERINA's *part is mute, but as she enters she stands by the fortepiano and energetically mimes her rapturous singing. At the keyboard, old* BONNO· *accompanies her appreciatively.*]

She was later to become the best singer of her age. But at that time she was mainly a bubbling student with merry eyes and a sweet, eatable mouth. I was very much in love with Katherina—or at least in lust. But because of my vow to God I was entirely faithful to my wife. I had never laid a finger upon the girl—except occasionally to depress her diaphragm in the way of teaching her to sing. My ambition burned with an unquenchable flame. Its chief goal was the post of First Royal Kapellmeister, then held by Giuseppe Bonno [*Indicating him*], seventy years old, and apparently immortal.

[*All on stage, save* SALIERI, *suddenly freeze. He speaks very directly to the audience.*]

You, when you come, will be told that we musicians of the eighteenth century were no better than servants: the willing slaves of the well-to-do. This is quite true. It is also quite false. Yes, we were servants. But we were learned servants! And we used our learning to celebrate men's average lives.

[*A grander music sounds. The* EMPEROR *remains seated, but the other four men in the Light Box*—STRACK, ROSENBERG, VAN SWIETEN *and the* PRIEST—*come slowly out onto the main stage and process imposingly down it, and around it, and up it again to return to their places. Only the* PRIEST *goes off, as do* TERESA *on her side, and* KATHERINA *on hers.*]

[*Over this*] We took unremarkable men— usual bankers, run-of-the-mill priests, ordinary soldiers and statesmen and wives—and sacramentalized their mediocrity. We smoothed their noons with strings *divisi!* We pierced their nights with *chitarrini!* We gave them processions for their strutting, serenades for their rutting, high horns for their hunting, and drums for their wars! Trumpets sounded when they entered the world, and trombones groaned when they left it! The savor of their days remains behind because of us, our music still remembered while their politics are long forgotten.

[*The* EMPEROR *hands his rolled paper to* STRACK *and goes off. In the Light Box are left standing, like three icons,* ORSINI-ROSEN-BERG, *plump and supercilious, aged sixty;* VON STRACK, *stiff and proper, aged fifty-*

five; VAN SWIETEN, *cultivated and serious, aged fifty. The lights go down on them a little.]*

Tell me, before you call us servants, who served whom? And who, I wonder, in your generations, will immortalize you?

[The two VENTICELLI *come on quickly downstage, from either side. They are now bewigged also, and are dressed well, in the style of the late eighteenth century. Their manner is more confidential than before.]*

V.1: [To SALIERI]. Sir!

V.2: [To SALIERI]. Sir!

V.1: Sir. Sir.

V.2: Sir. Sir. Sir!

[SALIERI bids them wait for a second.]

SALIERI: I was the most successful young musician in the city of musicians. And now suddenly, without warning—

[They approach him eagerly, from either side.]

V.1: Mozart!

V.2: Mozart!

V.1 & V.2: *Mozart has come!*

SALIERI: These are my Venticelli. My "Little Winds," as I called them. *[He gives each a coin from his pocket.]* The secret of successful living in a large city is always to know to the minute what is being done behind your back.

V.1: He's left Salzburg.

V.2: Means to give concerts.

V.1: Asking for subscribers.

SALIERI: I'd known of him for years, of course. Tales of his prowess were told all over Europe.

V.1: They say he wrote his first symphony at five.

V.2: I hear his first concerto at four.

V.1: A full opera at fourteen!

SALIERI: [To them]. How old is he now?

V.2: Twenty-five.

SALIERI: [Carefully]. And how long is he remaining?

V.1: He's not departing.

V.2: He's here to stay.

> [The VENTICELLI glide off.]

SCENE 4

The Palace of Schönbrunn

Lights come up on the three stiff figures of ROSENBERG, STRACK *and* VAN SWIETEN, *standing upstage in the Light Box. The* CHAMBERLAIN *hands the paper he has received from* the EMPEROR to the DIRECTOR OF THE OPERA. SALIERI remains downstage.]

STRACK: [To ROSENBERG]. You are required to commission a comic opera in German from Herr Mozart.

SALIERI: [To audience]. Johann von Strack. Royal Chamberlain. A court official to his collarbone.

ROSENBERG: [Loftily]. Why in German? Italian is the only possible language for opera!

SALIERI: Count Orsini-Rosenberg. Director of the Opera. Benevolent to all things Italian— especially myself.

STRACK: [Stiffly]. The idea of a national opera is dear to His Majesty's heart. He desires to hear pieces in good plain German.

VAN SWIETEN: Yes, but why comic? It is not the function of music to be funny.

SALIERI: Baron van Swieten. Prefect of the Imperial Library. Ardent Freemason. Yet to find anything funny. Known, for his enthusiasm for old-fashioned music, as "Lord Fugue."

VAN SWIETEN: I heard last week a remarkable serious opera from Mozart: Idomeneo, King of Crete.

ROSENBERG: I heard that too. A young fellow trying to impress beyond his abilities. Too much spice. Too many notes.

STRACK: [Firmly, to ROSENBERG]. Nevertheless, kindly convey the commission to him today.

ROSENBERG: [Taking the paper reluctantly]. I

believe we are going to have trouble with this young man.

[ROSENBERG *leaves the Light Box and strolls down the stage to* SALIERI.]

He was a child prodigy. That always spells trouble. His father is Leopold Mozart, a bad-tempered Salzburg musician who dragged the boy endlessly round Europe, making him play the keyboard blindfolded, with one finger, and that sort of thing. [To SALIERI] All prodigies are hateful—non è vero, Compositore?

SALIERI: *Divengono sempre sterili con gli anni.*

ROSENBERG: *Precisamente. Precisamente.*

STRACK: [*Calling suspiciously*]. What are you saying?

ROSENBERG: [*Airily*]. Nothing, Herr Chamberlain! . . . Niente, Signor Pomposo! . . .

[*He strolls on out.* STRACK *strides off, irritated.* VAN SWIETEN *now comes down-stage.*]

VAN SWIETEN: We meet tomorrow, I believe, on your committee to devise pensions for old musicians.

SALIERI: [*Deferentially*]. It's most gracious of you to attend, Baron.

VAN SWIETEN: You're a worthy man, Salieri. You should join our Brotherhood of Masons. We would welcome you warmly.

SALIERI: I would be honored, Baron!

VAN SWIETEN: If you wished, I could arrange initiation into my lodge.

SALIERI: That would be more than my due.

VAN SWIETEN: Nonsense. We embrace men of talent of all conditions. I may invite young Mozart also—dependent on the impression he makes.

SALIERI: [Bowing]. Of course, Baron.

[VAN SWIETEN goes out.]

[To audience] Honor indeed. In those days almost every man of influence in Vienna was a Mason, and the Baron's lodge by far the most fashionable. As for young Mozart, I confess I was alarmed by his coming. Not by the commission of a comic opera, even though I myself was then attempting one called The Chimney Sweep. No, what worried me were reports about the man himself. He was praised altogether too much.

[The VENTICELLI hurry in from either side.]

V.1: Such gaiety of spirit!

V.2: Such ease of manner!

V.1: Such natural charm!

SALIERI: [To the VENTICELLI]. Really? Where does he live?

V.1: Peter Platz.

V.2: Number eleven.

V.1: The landlady is Madame Weber.

V.2: A real bitch.

V.1: Takes in male lodgers, and has a tribe of daughters.

V.2: Mozart is after one of them.

V.1: Constanze.

V.2: Flighty little piece.

V.1: Her mother's pushing marriage.

V.2: His *father* isn't!

V.1: Daddy is worried sick!

V.2: Writes him every day from Salzburg!

SALIERI: [*To them*]. I want to meet him. What houses does he visit?

V.1: He'll be at the Baroness Waldstädten's tomorrow night.

SALIERI: *Grazie.*

V.2: Some of his music is to be played.

SALIERI: [*To both*]. *Restiamo in contatto.*

V.1 & V.2: *Certamente, Signore!*
   [*They go off.*]

SALIERI: [*To audience*]. So to the Baroness Waldstädten's I went. That night changed my life.

SCENE 5

The Library of the Baroness
Waldstädten

[In the Light Box, two elegantly curtained windows surrounded by handsome subdued wallpaper.

Two SERVANTS bring on a large table loaded with cakes and desserts. Two more carry on a grand high-backed wing chair, which they place ceremoniously downstage at the left.]

SALIERI: [To audience]. I entered the library to take first a little refreshment. My generous hostess always put out the most delicious confections in that room whenever she knew I was coming. *Dolci, caramelli,* and most especially a miraculous *crema al mascarpone*—which is simply cream cheese mixed with granulated sugar and suffused with rum—that was totally irresistible!

[He takes a little bowl of it from the cake-

stand and sits in the wing chair, facing out front. Thus seated, he is invisible to anyone entering from upstage.]

I had just sat down in a high-backed chair to consume this paradisal dish—unobservable, as it happened, to anyone who might come in.

[Offstage, noises are heard.]

CONSTANZE: *[Off]*. Squeak! Squeak! Squeak!

[CONSTANZE runs on from upstage: a pretty girl in her early twenties, full of high spirits. At this second she is pretending to be a mouse. She runs across the stage in her gay party dress, and hides under the forte-piano.

Suddenly a small, pallid, large-eyed man in a showy wig and a showy set of clothes runs in after her and freezes—center—as a cat would freeze, hunting a mouse. This is WOLFGANG AMADEUS MOZART.

As we get to know him through his next scenes, we discover several things about him: he is an extremely restless man, his hands and feet in almost continuous motion; his voice is light and high; and he is possessed of an unforgettable giggle—piercing and infantile.]

MOZART: Miaouw!

CONSTANZE: *[Betraying where she is]*. Squeak!

MOZART: Miaouw! . . . Miaouw! . . . Miaouw!

[The composer drops on all fours and, wrin-

kling his face, begins spitting and stalking his prey. The mouse—giggling with excitement—breaks her cover and dashes across the floor. The cat pursues. Almost at the chair where SALIERI sits concealed, the mouse turns at bay. The cat stalks her—nearer and nearer—in its knee breeches and elaborate coat.]

I'm going to pounce-bounce! I'm going to scrunch-munch! I'm going to chew-poo my little mouse-wouse! I'm going to tear her to bits with my paws-claws!

CONSTANZE: No!

MOZART: Paws-claws—paws-claws—paws-claws! *Ohh!*

[*He falls on her. She screams.*]

SALIERI: [*To audience*]. Before I could rise, it had become difficult to do so.

MOZART: I'm going to bite you in half with my fangs-wangs! My little Stanzerl-wanzerl-banzerl!

[*She laughs delightedly, lying prone beneath him.*]

You're trembling! . . . I think you're frightened of puss-wuss! . . . I think you're scared to death! [*Intimately*] I think you're going to shit yourself!

[*She squeals, but is not really shocked. He emits a high-pitched giggle.*]

In a moment it's going to be on the floor!

CONSTANZE: Sssh! Someone'll hear you!
   [*He imitates the noise of a fart.*]
   Stop it, Wolferl! Ssh!
MOZART: Here it comes now! I can hear it
   coming! . . . Oh, what a melancholy note!
   Something's dropping from your boat!
   [*Another fart noise, slower.* CONSTANZE
   shrieks with amusement.]
CONSTANZE: Stop it now! It's stupid! Really
   stupid!
   [SALIERI *sits appalled.*]
MOZART: Hey—hey—what's "Trazom"?
CONSTANZE: What?
MOZART: T-r-a-z-o-m. What's that mean?
CONSTANZE: How should *I* know?
MOZART: It's Mozart spelled backwards—shit-
   wit! If you ever married me, you'd be Con-
   stanze Trazom.
CONSTANZE: No, I wouldn't.
MOZART: Yes, you would. Because I'd want ev-
   erything backwards once I was married. I'd
   want to lick my wife's arse instead of her
   face.
CONSTANZE: You're not going to lick anything
   at this rate. Your father's never going to give
   his consent to us.
   [*The sense of fun deserts him instantly.*]
MOZART: And who cares about his consent?
CONSTANZE: You do. You care very much. You
   wouldn't do it without it.

MOZART: Wouldn't I?

CONSTANZE: No, you wouldn't. Because you're too scared of him. I know what he says about me. [Solemn voice] "If you marry that dreadful girl, you'll end up lying on straw with beggars for children!"

MOZART: [Impulsively]. Marry me!

CONSTANZE: Don't be silly.

MOZART: Marry me!

CONSTANZE: Are you serious?

MOZART: [Defiantly]. Yes! . . . Answer me this minute: yes or no! Say yes, then I can go home, climb into bed, shit over the mattress and shout, "I did it!"

[He rolls on top of her delightedly, uttering his high whinnying giggle. The MAJORDOMO of the house stalks in, upstage.]

MAJORDOMO: [Imperviously]. Her Ladyship is ready to commence.

MOZART: Ah! . . . Yes! . . . Good! [He picks himself up, embarrassed, and helps CONSTANZE to rise. With an attempt at dignity] Come, my dear. The music waits!

CONSTANZE: [Suppressing giggles]. Oh, by all means—Herr Trazom!

[He takes her arm. They prance off together, followed by the disapproving MAJORDOMO. SALIERI sits shaken.]

SALIERI: [To audience]. And then, right away, the concert began. I heard it through the door—some serenade—at first only vaguely, too horrified to attend. But presently the sound insisted—a solemn Adagio in E flat.

[*The Adagio from the Serenade for thirteen wind instruments (K. 361) begins to sound. Quietly and quite slowly, seated in the wing chair,* SALIERI *speaks over the music.*]

SALIERI: It started simply enough: just a pulse in the lowest registers—bassoons and basset horns—like a rusty squeezebox. It would have been comic except for the slowness, which gave it instead a sort of serenity. And then suddenly, high above it, sounded a single note on the oboe.

[*We hear it.*]

It hung there unwavering, piercing me through, till breath could hold it no longer, and a clarinet withdrew it out of me, and sweetened it into a phrase of such delight it had me trembling. The light flickered in the room. My eyes clouded! [*With ever-increasing emotion and vigor*] The squeezebox groaned louder, and over it the higher instruments wailed and warbled, throwing lines of sound around me—long lines of pain around and through me. Ah, the pain! Pain as I had never known it. I called up to my sharp old God, "What is this? . . . What?!" But the squeezebox went on and on, and the pain cut deeper

into my shaking head, until suddenly I was
running—

[He bolts out of the chair and runs across
the stage in a fever, to a corner, down
right. Behind him in the Light Box, the
library fades into a street scene at night:
small houses under a rent sky. The music
continues, fainter, underneath.]

dashing through the side door, stumbling
downstairs into the street, into the cold night,
gasping for life. [Calling up in agony] "What?!
What is this? Tell me, Signore! What is this
pain? What is this need in the sound? Forever
unfulfillable, yet fulfilling him who hears it,
utterly. Is it Your need? Can it be Yours? . . ."

[Pause]

Dimly the music sounded from the salon
above. Dimly the stars shone on the empty
street. I was suddenly frightened. It seemed
to me that I had heard a voice of God—and
that it issued from a creature whose own
voice I had also heard—and it was the voice
of an obscene child!

[Light change. The street scene fades.]

SCENE 6

Salieri's Apartment

[*It remains dark.*]

SALIERI: I ran home and buried my fear in work. More pupils—till there were thirty and forty. More committees to help musicians. More motets and anthems to God's glory. And at night I prayed for just one thing. [*He kneels desperately.*] "Let your voice enter *me!* Let me conduct you! ... *Let* me!" [*Pause. He rises.*] As for Mozart, I avoided meeting him— and sent out my Little Winds for whatever scores of his could be found.

[*The* VENTICELLI *come in with manuscripts.* SALIERI *sits at the fortepiano, and they show him the music alternately, as* SERVANTS *unobtrusively remove the Waldstädten table and wing chair.*]

V.1: Six fortepiano sonatas composed in Munich.

V.2: Two in Mannheim.

V.1: A Parisian symphony.

SALIERI: [*To audience*]. Clever. They were all clever. But yet they seemed to me completely empty!

V.1: A Divertimento in D.

V.2: A Cassazione in G.

V.1: A Grand Litany in E Flat.

SALIERI: [*To audience*]. The same. Conventional. Even boring. The productions of a precocious youngster—Leopold Mozart's swanky son— nothing more. That Serenade was obviously an exception in his work: the sort of accident which might visit any composer on a lucky day!

[*The* VENTICELLI *go off with the music.*]

Had I in fact been simply taken by surprise that the filthy creature could write music at all? . . . Suddenly I felt immensely cheered! I would seek him out and welcome him myself to Vienna!

SCENE 7

The Palace of Schönbrunn

[Quick light change. The EMPEROR is revealed standing in bright light before the gilded mirrors and the fireplace, attended by CHAMBERLAIN STRACK. His Majesty is a dapper, cheerful figure, aged forty, largely pleased with himself and the world. Downstage, from opposite sides, VAN SWIETEN and ROSENBERG hurry on.]

JOSEPH: Fêtes and fireworks, gentlemen! Mozart is here! He's waiting below!

[All bow.]

ALL: Majesty!

JOSEPH: Je suis follement impatient!

SALIERI: [To audience]. The Emperor Joseph the Second of Austria. Son of Maria Theresa. Brother of Marie Antoinette. Adorer of music—provided that it made no demands upon the royal brain. [To the EMPEROR, deferentially] Majesty, I have written a little march in Mozart's honor. May I play it as he comes in?

JOSEPH: By all means, Court Composer. What a delightful idea! Have you met him yet?

SALIERI: Not yet, Majesty.

JOSEPH: Fêtes and fireworks, what fun! Strack, bring him up at once.

[STRACK goes off. The EMPEROR comes onto the stage proper.]

Mon Dieu, I wish we could have a competition! Mozart against some other virtuoso. Two keyboards in contest. Wouldn't that be fun, Baron?

VAN SWIETEN: [Stiffly]. Not to me, Majesty. In my view, musicians are not horses to be run against one another.

[Slight pause]

JOSEPH: Ah. Well—there it is.

[STRACK returns.]

STRACK: Herr Mozart, Majesty.

JOSEPH: Ah! Splendid! . . . [Conspiratorially he signs to SALIERI, who moves quickly to the fortepiano.] Court Composer—allons! [To STRACK] Admit him, please.

[Instantly SALIERI sits at the instrument and strikes up his march on the keyboard. At the same moment MOZART struts in, wearing an extremely ornate surcoat, with dress sword. The EMPEROR stands downstage, center, his back to the audience, and as MOZART approaches he signs to him to halt and listen. Bewildered, MOZART does so,

33

becoming *aware of* SALIERI *playing his March of Welcome. It is an extremely banal piece, vaguely—but only vaguely— reminiscent of another march to become very famous later on. All stand frozen in attitudes of listening, until* SALIERI *comes to a finish. Applause.*]

JOSEPH: [*To* SALIERI]. Charming . . . *Comme d'habitude!* [*He turns and extends his hand to be kissed.*] Mozart.

[MOZART *approaches and kneels extravagantly.*]

MOZART: Majesty! Your Majesty's humble slave! Let me kiss your royal hand a hundred thousand times!

[*He kisses it greedily, over and over, until its owner withdraws it in embarrassment.*]

JOSEPH: *Non, non, s'il vous plaît!* A little less enthusiasm, I beg you. Come sir, *levez-vous!* [*He assists* MOZART *to rise.*] You will not recall it, but the last time we met, you were also on the floor! My sister remembers it to this day. This young man—all of six years old, mind you—slipped on the floor at Schönbrunn—came a nasty purler on his little head. . . . Have I told you this before?

ROSENBERG: [*Hastily*]. No, Majesty!

STRACK: [*Hastily*]. No, Majesty!

SALIERI: [*Hastily*]. No, Majesty!

JOSEPH: Well, my sister Antoinette runs for-

ward and picks him up herself. And do you
know what he does? Jumps right into her
arms—hoopla, just like that!—kisses her on
both cheeks and says, "Will you marry me:
yes or no?"

[*The* COURTIERS *laugh politely.* MOZART
emits his high-pitched giggle. The EMPEROR
is clearly startled by it.]

I do not mean to embarrass you, Herr Mozart.
You know everyone here, surely?

MOZART: Yes, sire. [*Bowing elaborately. To*
ROSENBERG] Herr Director! [*To* VAN SWIETEN]
Herr Prefect.

VAN SWIETEN: [*Warmly*]. Delighted to see you
again!

JOSEPH: But not, I think, our esteemed Court
Composer! . . . A most serious omission! No
one who cares for art can afford not to know
Herr Salieri. He wrote that exquisite little
March of Welcome for you.

SALIERI: It was a trifle, Majesty.

JOSEPH: Nevertheless . . .

MOZART: [*To* SALIERI]. I'm overwhelmed, Signore!

JOSEPH: Ideas simply pour out of him—don't
they, Strack?

STRACK: Endlessly, Sire. [*As if tipping him*] Well
done, Salieri.

JOSEPH: Let it be my pleasure then to introduce
you. Court Composer Salieri—Herr Mozart of
Salzburg.

35

SALIERI: [*Sleekly, to* MOZART]. *Finalmente. Che gioia. Che diletto straordinario.*

[*He gives him a prim bow and presents the copy of his music to the other composer, who accepts it with a flood of Italian.*]

MOZART: *Grazie, Signore! Mille milione di benvenuti! Sono commosso! E un onore eccezionale incontrare! Compositore brillante e famosissimo!* [*He makes an elaborate and showy bow in return.*]

SALIERI: [*Dryly*]. *Grazie.*

JOSEPH: Tell me, Mozart, have you received our commission for the opera?

MOZART: Indeed I have, Majesty! I am so grateful I can hardly speak! . . . I swear to you that you will have the best, the most perfect entertainment ever offered a monarch. I've already found a libretto.

ROSENBERG: [*Startled*]. Have you? I didn't hear of this!

MOZART: Forgive me, Herr Director, I entirely omitted to tell you.

ROSENBERG: May I ask why?

MOZART: It didn't seem very important.

ROSENBERG: Not important?

MOZART: Not really, no.

ROSENBERG: [*Irritated*]. It is important to *me*, Herr Mozart.

MOZART [*Embarrassed*]. Yes, I see that. Of course.

ROSENBERG: And who, pray, is it by?

MOZART: Stephanie.

ROSENBERG: A most unpleasant man.

MOZART: But a brilliant writer.

ROSENBERG: Do you think?

MOZART: The story is really amusing, Majesty. The whole plot is set in a—[*He giggles*]—in a . . .

JOSEPH: [*Eagerly*]. Where? Where is it set?

MOZART: It's—it's rather saucy, Majesty!

JOSEPH: Yes, yes! Where?

MOZART: Well, it's actually set in a *seraglio*.

JOSEPH: A what?

MOZART: A pasha's harem. [*He giggles wildly.*]

ROSENBERG: And you imagine that is a suitable subject for performance at a national theater?

MOZART: [*In a panic*]. Yes! . . . No! . . . Yes, I mean yes, yes I do. Why not? It's very funny, it's amusing. . . . On my honor, Majesty, there's nothing offensive in it. Nothing offensive in the world. It's full of proper German virtues, I swear it!

SALIERI: [*Blandly*]. Scusate, Signore, but what are those? Being a foreigner, I'm not sure.

JOSEPH: You are being *cattivo*, Court Composer.

SALIERI: Not at all, Majesty.

JOSEPH: Come then, Mozart. Name us a proper German virtue!

MOZART: Love, Sire. I have yet to see that expressed in any opera.

37

VAN SWIETEN: Well answered, Mozart.

SALIERI: [*Smiling*]. *Scusate*. I was under the impression one rarely saw anything *else* expressed in opera.

MOZART: I mean manly love, Signore. Not male sopranos screeching. Or stupid couples rolling their eyes. All that absurd Italian rubbish.

[*Pause. Tension.* ROSENBERG *coughs.*]

I mean the real thing.

JOSEPH: And do you know the real thing yourself, Herr Mozart?

MOZART: Under your pardon, I think I do, Majesty. [*He gives a short high giggle.*]

JOSEPH: Bravo. When do you think it will be done?

MOZART: The first act is already finished.

JOSEPH: But it can't be more than two weeks since you started!

MOZART: Composing is not hard when you have the right audience to please, Sire.

VAN SWIETEN: A charming reply, Majesty.

JOSEPH: Indeed, Baron. Fêtes and fireworks! I see we are going to have fêtes and fireworks! *Au revoir, Monsieur Mozart. Soyez bienvenu à la court.*

MOZART: [*With expert rapidity*]. *Majesté! Je suis comblé d'honneur d'être accepté dans la maison du Père de tous les musiciens! Servir un monarque aussi plein de discernement que*

38

votre Majesté, c'est un honneur qui dépasse
le sommet de mes dûs!

[A pause. The EMPEROR is taken aback by
this flood of French.]

JOSEPH: Ah. Well—there it is! I'll leave you
gentlemen to get better acquainted.

SALIERI: Good day, Majesty.

MOZART: Votre Majesté.

[They both bow. JOSEPH goes out.]

ROSENBERG: Good day to you.

STRACK: Good day.

[They follow the King.]

VAN SWIETEN: [Warmly shaking his hand]. Welcome, Mozart. I shall see much more of you.
Depend on it!

MOZART: Thank you.

[He bows. The BARON goes. MOZART and
SALIERI are left alone.]

SALIERI: Bene.

MOZART: Bene.

SALIERI: I, too, wish you success with your opera.

MOZART: I'll have it. It's going to be superb. I
must tell you I have already found the most
excellent singer for the leading part.

SALIERI: Oh? Who is that?

MOZART: Her name is Cavalieri. Katherina Cavalieri. She's really German, but she thinks it
will advance her career if she sports an Italian
name.

SALIERI: She's quite right. It was my idea. She is

in fact my prize pupil. Actually she's a very innocent child. Silly in the way of young singers—but, you know, she's only twenty.

MOZART: Yes.

[*Without emphasis,* MOZART *freezes his movements and* SALIERI *takes one easy step forward to make a fluent aside.*]

[*To audience*] I had kept my hands off Katherina. Yes! But I could not bear to think of anyone else's upon her—least of all his!

MOZART: [*Unfreezing*]. You're a good fellow, Salieri! And that's a jolly little thing you wrote for me.

SALIERI: It was my pleasure.

MOZART: Let's see if I can remember it. May I?

SALIERI: By all means. It's yours.

MOZART: Grazie, Signore.

[MOZART *tosses the manuscript onto the lid of the fortepiano, where he cannot see it, sits at the instrument, and plays* SALIERI's *March of Welcome perfectly from memory— at first slowly, recalling it, but on the reprise of the tune, very much faster.*]

The rest is just the same, isn't it? [*He finishes it with insolent speed.*]

SALIERI: You have a remarkable memory.

MOZART: [*Delighted with himself*]. Grazie ancora, Signore! [*He plays the opening seven bars again, but this time stops on the interval of the fourth, and sounds it again with dis-*

pleasure.] It doesn't really work, that fourth, does it? . . . Let's try the third above. . . . [He does so—and smiles happily.] Ah yes! . . . Good!

[He repeats the new interval, leading up to it smartly with the well-known military-trumpet arpeggio which characterizes the celebrated March from The Marriage of Figaro, "Non più andrai." Then, using the interval—tentatively, delicately, one note at a time, in the treble—he steals into the famous tune itself.

On and on he plays, improvising happily what is virtually the March we know now, laughing gleefully each time he comes to the amended interval of a third. SALIERI watches him with an answering smile painted on his face.

MOZART's playing grows more and more exhibitionistic, revealing to the audience the formidable virtuoso he is. The whole time he himself remains totally oblivious of the offense he is giving. Finally, he finishes the march with a series of triumphant flourishes and chords.

An ominous pause.]

SALIERI: Scusate. I must go.

MOZART: Really? [Springing up and indicating the keyboard] Why don't you try a variation?

SALIERI: Thank you, but I must attend on the Emperor.

MOZART: Ah.

SALIERI: It has been delightful to meet you.

MOZART: For me too! ... And thanks for the march!

[MOZART *picks up the manuscript from the top of the fortepiano and marches happily offstage. A slight pause.* SALIERI *moves toward the audience. The lights go down around him.*]

SALIERI: [*To audience*]. Was it then—so early— that I began to have thoughts of murder? ... Of course not: at least not in life. In art it was a different matter. I decided I would compose a huge tragic opera: something to astonish the world! And I knew my theme. I would set the legend of Danaius, who, for a monstrous crime, was chained to a rock for eternity, his head repeatedly struck by lightning! Wickedly in my head I saw Mozart in that position. ... In reality, of course, the man was in no danger from me at all. ... Not yet.

SCENE 8

The First Performance of
The Abduction from the Seraglio

[The light changes, and the stage instantly
turns into an eighteenth-century theater. The
backdrop projection shows a line of softly
gleaming chandeliers.

The SERVANTS bring in chairs and benches.
Upon them, facing the audience and re-
garding it as if watching an opera, sit the
EMPEROR JOSEPH, STRACK, ROSENBERG and
VAN SWIETEN. Next to them: KAPELLMEISTER
BONNO and THERESA SALIERI. A little be-
hind them: CONSTANZE. Behind her: CITIZENS
OF VIENNA.]

SALIERI: The first performance of *The Abduction from the Seraglio.* The creature's expression of manly love.

[MOZART comes on briskly, wearing a gaudy
new coat embellished with scarlet ribbons,
and a new powdered wig. He struts quickly

43

> *to the fortepiano, sits at it and mimes conducting.* SALIERI *sits nearby, next to his wife, and watches* MOZART *intently.*]

He himself contrived to wear for the occasion an even more vulgar coat than usual. As for the music, it matched the coat completely. For my dear pupil Katherina Cavalieri he had written quite simply the showiest Aria I'd ever heard

> [*Faintly we hear the whizzing scale passages for soprano which end the aria "Martern aller arten."*]

Ten minutes of scales and ornaments, amounting in sum to a vast emptiness. So ridiculous was the piece, in fact—so much what might be demanded by a foolish young soprano—that I knew precisely what Mozart must have demanded in return for it.

> [*The final orchestral chords of the aria. Silence. No one moves.*]

Although engaged to be married, he'd had her! I knew that beyond any doubt. [*Bluntly*] The creature had had my darling girl.

> [*Loudly we heard the brilliant Turkish finale of* Seraglio. *Great applause from those watching.* MOZART *jumps to his feet and acknowledges it. The* EMPEROR *rises—as do all—and gestures graciously to the "stage" in invitation.* KATHERINA CAVALIERI *runs on in her costume, all plumes and flounces,*

44

to renewed cheering and clapping. She curtsies to the EMPEROR—is kissed by SALIERI—
presented to his wife—curtsies again to
MOZART and, flushed with triumph, moves
to one side.

In the ensuing brief silence, CONSTANZE
rushes down from the back, wildly excited.
She flings herself on MOZART, not even no-
ticing the EMPEROR.]

CONSTANZE: Oh, well done, lovey! . . . Well
done, pussy-wussy! . . .

[MOZART indicates the proximity of His
Majesty.]

Oh! . . . 'Scuse me! [She curtsies in embarrassment.]

MOZART: Majesty, may I present my fiancée,
Fräulein Weber.

JOSEPH: Enchanté, Fräulein.

CONSTANZE: Your Majesty!

MOZART: Constanze is a singer herself.

JOSEPH: Indeed?

CONSTANZE: [Embarrassed]. I'm not at all,
Majesty. Don't be silly, Wolfgang!

JOSEPH: So, Mozart—a good effort. Decidedly
that. A good effort.

MOZART: Did you really like it, Sire?

JOSEPH: I thought it was most interesting. Yes,
indeed. A trifle . . . how shall one say? [To
ROSENBERG] How shall one say, Director?

ROSENBERG: [*Subserviently*]. Too many notes, Your Majesty?

JOSEPH: Very well put. Too many notes.

MOZART: I don't understand.

JOSEPH: My dear fellow, don't take it too hard. There are in fact only so many notes the ear can hear in the course of an evening. I think I'm right in saying that, aren't I, Court Composer?

SALIERI: [*Uncomfortably*]. Well, yes, I would say yes, on the whole, yes, Majesty.

JOSEPH: There you are. It's clever. It's German. It's quality work. And there are simply too many notes. Do you see?

MOZART: There are just as many notes, Majesty, neither more nor less, as are required.

[*Pause*]

JOSEPH: Ah . . . Well—there it is! [*He goes off abruptly, followed by* ROSENBERG *and* STRACK.]

MOZART: [*Nervously*]. Is he angry?

SALIERI: Not at all. He respects you for your views.

MOZART: I hope so. . . . What did you think yourself, sir? Did you care for the piece at all?

SALIERI: Yes, of course, Mozart—at its best, it is truly charming.

MOZART: And at other times?

SALIERI: [*Smoothly*]. Well, just occasionally, at other times—in Katherina's aria, for example— it was a little excessive.

46

MOZART: Katherina is an excessive girl. In fact, she's insatiable. . . . I mean in regard to vocal ornaments.

SALIERI: All the same, as my revered teacher the Chevalier Gluck used to say to me, one must avoid music that smells of music.

MOZART: What does that mean?

SALIERI: Music which makes one aware too much of the virtuosity of the composer.

MOZART: Gluck is absurd.

SALIERI: What do you say?

MOZART: He's talked all his life about moderniz-ing opera, but creates people so lofty they sound as though they shit marble.

[CONSTANZE *gives a little scream of shock.*]

CONSTANZE: Oh, 'scuse me! . . .

MOZART: [*Breaking out*]. No, but it's too much! . . . Gluck says! Gluck says! Chevalier Gluck! . . . What's Chevalier? I'm a Chevalier. The Pope made me a Chevalier when I was still wetting my bed.

CONSTANZE: Wolfel!

MOZART: Anyway, it's ridiculous. Only stupid farts sport titles.

SALIERI: [*Blandly*]. Such as Court Composer?

MOZART: What? . . . [*Realizing*] Ah. Oh. Ha. Ha. Well! . . . My father's right again. He always tells me I should padlock my mouth. . . . Actually, I shouldn't speak at all!

SALIERI: [*Soothingly*]. Nonsense. I'm just being

what the Emperor would call *cattivo*. Won't
you introduce me to your charming fiancée?

MOZART: Oh, of course! Constanze, this is Herr
Salieri, the Court Composer. Fräulein Weber.

SALIERI: [*Bowing*]. Delighted, *cara Fräulein*.

CONSTANZE: [*Bobbing*]. How do you do, Excellency?

SALIERI: May I ask when you marry?

MOZART: [*Nervously*]. We have to secure my
father's consent. He's an excellent man—a
wonderful man—but in some ways a little
stubborn.

SALIERI: Excuse me, but how old are you?

MOZART: Twenty-six.

SALIERI: Then your father's consent is scarcely
indispensable.

CONSTANZE: [To MOZART]. You see?

MOZART: [*Uncomfortably*]. Well, no, it's not
indispensable—of course not! . . .

SALIERI: My advice to you is to marry and be
happy. You have found—it's quite obvious—
un tesoro raro!

CONSTANZE: Ta very much.

SALIERI: [*He kisses* CONSTANZE's *hand. She is
delighted.*] Good night to you both.

CONSTANZE: Good night, Excellency!

MOZART: Good night, sir. And thank you . . .
Come, Stanzerl.

[*They depart delightedly. He watches them
go.*]

SALIERI: [To audience]. As I watched her walk away on the arm of the creature, I felt the lightning thought strike: "Have her! Her for Katherina!" ... Abomination! ... Never in my life had I entertained a notion so sinful!

[Light change: the eighteenth century fades. The VENTICELLI come on merrily, as if from some celebration. One holds a bottle; the other, a glass.]

V.1: They're married.

SALIERI: [To them]. What?

V.2: Mozart and Weber—married!

SALIERI: Really?

V.1: His father will be furious!

V.2: They didn't even wait for his consent!

SALIERI: Have they set up house?

V.1: Wipplingerstrasse.

V.2: Number twelve.

V.1: Not bad.

V.2: Considering they've no money.

SALIERI: Is that really true?

V.1: He's wildly extravagant.

V.2: Lives way beyond his means.

SALIERI: But he has pupils.

V.1: Only three.

SALIERI: [To them]. Why so few?

V.1: He's embarrassing.

V.2: Makes scenes.

V.1: Makes enemies.

49

V.2: Even Strack, whom he cultivates.
SALIERI: Chamberlain Strack?
V.1: Only last night.
V.2: At Kapellmeister Bonno's.

SCENE 9

Bonno's Salon

[*Instant light change.* MOZART *comes in with* STRACK. *He is high on wine, and holding a glass. The* VENTICELLI *join the scene, but still talk out of it to Salieri. One of them fills* MOZART's *glass.*]

MOZART: Seven months in this city and not one job! I'm not to be tried again, is that it?
STRACK: Of course not.
MOZART: I know what goes on, and so do you. Germany is completely in the hands of foreigners. Worthless wops like *Kapellmeister Bonno!*
STRACK: Please! You're in the man's house!
MOZART: Court Composer *Salieri!*
STRACK: Hush!

MOZART: Did you see his last opera—*The Chimney Sweep?* . . . Did you?

STRACK: Of course I did.

MOZART: Dogshit. Dried dogshit.

STRACK: [*Outraged*]. I beg your pardon!

MOZART: [*Singing*]. Pom-pom, pom-pom, pom-pom, pom-pom! Tonic and dominant, tonic and dominant, from here to resurrection! Not one interesting modulation all night. Salieri is a musical idiot!

STRACK: Please!

V.1: [*To* SALIERI]. He'd had too much to drink.

V.2: He often has.

MOZART: Why are Italians so terrified by the slightest complexity in music? Show them one chromatic passage and they *faint!* . . . "Oh, how sick! How morbid!" [*Falsetto*] *Morboso!* . . . *Nervoso!* . . . *Ohimè!* . . . No wonder the music at this court is so dreary.

STRACK: Lower your voice.

MOZART: Lower your breeches! . . . That's just a joke—just a joke!

[*Unobserved by him,* COUNT ROSENBERG *has entered upstage and is suddenly standing between the* VENTICELLI, *listening. He wears a waistcoat of bright green silk, and an expression of supercilious interest.* MOZART *sees him. A pause.*]

[*Pleasantly, to* ROSENBERG] You look like a

toad . . . I mean, you're goggling like a toad.
[*He emits his giggle.*]

ROSENBERG: [*Blandly*]. You would do best to
retire tonight, for your own sake.

MOZART: Salieri has fifty pupils. I have three.
How am I to live? I'm a married man now!
. . . Of course, I realize you don't concern
yourselves with money in these exalted circles.
All the same, did you know behind his back
His Majesty is known as Kaiser Keep-it? [*He
giggles wildly.*]

STRACK: *Mozart!*
[*He stops.*]

MOZART: I shouldn't have said that, should I?
. . . Forgive me. It was just a joke. Another
joke! . . . I can't help myself! . . . We're all
friends here, aren't we?
[*STRACK and ROSENBERG glare at him. Then
STRACK leaves abruptly, much offended.*]
What's wrong with him?

ROSENBERG: Good night. [*He turns to go.*]

MOZART: No, no, no—please! [*He grabs the
DIRECTOR's arm.*] Your hand please, first!
[*Unwillingly, ROSENBERG gives him his
hand. MOZART kisses it.*]
[*Humbly*] Give me a post, sir.

ROSENBERG: That is not in my power, Mozart.

MOZART: The Princess Elizabeth is looking for
an instructor. One word from you could secure it for me.

ROSENBERG: I regret that is solely in the recommendation of Court Composer Salieri. [*He disengages himself.*]

MOZART: Do you know I am better than any musician in Vienna? . . . Do you?

[*ROSENBERG leaves. MOZART calls after him.*]
Foppy-wops—I'm sick of them! Foppy-wops! . . . [*Suddenly he giggles to himself, like a child.*] Foppy—poppy—snoppy—toppy—hoppy . . . wops!

[*He hops offstage.*]

SALIERI: [*Watching him go*]. Barely one month later, that thought of revenge became more than thought!

SCENE 10

The Waldstädten Library

[*Two simultaneous shouts bring up the lights. Against the handsome wallpaper stand three masked figures: CONSTANZE, flanked on either side by the VENTICELLI. All three are guests at a party, and are playing a game of forfeits.*

53

Two SERVANTS *stand frozen, holding the
large wing chair between them. Two more
hold the big table of sweetmeats.*]

V.1: Forfeit! . . . Forfeit! . . .

V.2: Forfeit, Stanzerl! You've got to forfeit!

CONSTANZE: I won't.

V.1: You have to.

V.2: It's the game.

[*The* SERVANTS *unfreeze and set down the
furniture.* SALIERI *moves to the wing chair
and sits.*]

SALIERI: [*To audience*]. Once again—believe it
or not—I was in the same concealing chair in
the Baroness's library [*Taking a cup from the
little table*] and consuming the same delicious dessert.

V.1: You lost—now there's the penalty!

SALIERI: [*To audience*]. A party celebrating the
New Year's Eve. I was on my own—my dear
spouse, Teresa, visiting her parents in Italy.

CONSTANZE: Well, what? . . . What is it?

[VENTICELLO ONE *snatches up an old-fashioned round ruler from off the fortepiano.*]

V.1: I want to measure your calves.

CONSTANZE: Oooo!

V.1: Well?

CONSTANZE: Definitely not. You cheeky bugger!

V.1: Now come on!

V.2: You've got to let him, Stanzerl. All's fair in
love and forfeits.

CONSTANZE: No, it isn't—so you can both buzz off!

V.1: If you don't let me, you won't be allowed to play again.

CONSTANZE: Well, choose something else.

V.1: I've chosen that! Now get up on the table. Quick, quick! *Allez-oop!* [*Gleefully he shifts the plates of sweetmeats to the fortepiano.*]

CONSTANZE: Quick, then! . . . Before anyone sees! [*The two masked men lift the shrieking masked girl up onto the table.*]

V.1: Hold her, Friedrich.

CONSTANZE: I don't have to be held, thank you!

V.2: Yes, you do—that's part of the penalty. [*He holds her ankles firmly, while* VENTI-CELLO ONE *thrusts the ruler under her skirts and measures her legs. Excitedly,* SALIERI *reverses his position so that he can kneel in the wing chair and watch.* CONSTANZE *giggles delightedly, then becomes out-raged—or pretends to be.*]

CONSTANZE: Stop it! . . . Stop that! That's quite enough of that! [*She bends down and tries to slap him.*]

V.1: Seventeen inches—knee to ankle!

V.2: Let me do it! You hold her.

CONSTANZE: That's not fair!

V.2: Yes, it is. You lost to me too.

CONSTANZE: It's been done now! Let me *down!*

V.2: Hold her, Karl.

CONSTANZE: No! . . .

> [VENTICELLO ONE *holds her ankles.* VENTI-
> CELLO TWO *thrusts his head entirely under
> her skirts. She squeals.*]

No—stop it! . . . No! . . .

> [*In the middle of this undignified scene,*
> MOZART *comes rushing on, also masked.*]

MOZART: [*Outraged*]. Constanze!

> [*They freeze.* SALIERI *ducks back down and
> sits hidden in the chair.*]

Gentlemen, if you please.

CONSTANZE: It's only a game, Wolferl! . . .

V.1: We meant no harm, 'pon my word.

MOZART: [*Stiffly*]. Come down off that table,
please.

> [*They hand her down.*]

Thank you. We'll see you later.

V.2: Now look, Mozart, don't be pompous—

MOZART: Please excuse us now.

> [*They go. The little man is very angry. He
> tears off his mask.*]

[*To* CONSTANZE] Do you realize what you've
done?

CONSTANZE: No, what? . . . [*Flustered, she busies herself restoring the plates of sweetmeats
to the table.*]

MOZART: Just lost your reputation, that's all!
You're now a loose girl.

CONSTANZE: Don't be so stupid. [*She, too, removes her mask.*]

MOZART: You are a married woman, for God's sake!

CONSTANZE: And what of it?

MOZART: A young wife does not allow her legs to be handled in public. Couldn't you at least have measured your own ugly legs?

CONSTANZE: *What?*

MOZART: [*Raising his voice*]. Do you know what you've done?! ... You've shamed me, that's all! *Shamed* me!

CONSTANZE: Oh, don't be so ridiculous!

MOZART: Shamed me—in front of *them!*

CONSTANZE: [*Suddenly furious*]. *You?* Shamed *you?* ... That's a laugh! If there's any shame around, lovey, it's *mine!*

MOZART: What do you mean?

CONSTANZE: You've only had every pupil who ever came to you.

MOZART: That's not true.

CONSTANZE: Every single female pupil!

MOZART: Name them! *Name them!*

CONSTANZE: The Aurnhammer girl! The Rumbeck girl! Katherina Cavalieri—that sly little whore! *She* wasn't even your pupil—she was Salieri's. Which actually, my dear, may be why he has hundreds and you have none. He doesn't drag them into bed!

MOZART: Of course he doesn't! He can't get it up, that's why! ... Have you heard his music?

That's the sound of someone who can't get it up! At least I can do that!

CONSTANZE: I'm sick of you!

MOZART: [Shouting]. No one ever said I couldn't do that!

CONSTANZE: [Bursting into tears]. I don't give a fart! I hate you! I hate you for ever and ever—I hate you! [A tiny pause. She weeps.]

MOZART: [Helplessly]. Oh, Stanzerl, don't cry. Please don't cry. . . . I can't bear it when you cry. I just didn't want you to look cheap in people's eyes, that's all. Here! [He snatches up the ruler.] Beat me. Beat me. . . . I'm your slave. Stanzi marini. Stanzi marini bini gini. I'll just stand here like a little lamb and bear your strokes. Here. Do it . . . Batti.

CONSTANZE: No.

MOZART: Batti, batti. Mio tesoro!

CONSTANZE: No!

MOZART: Stanzerly wanzerly piggly poo!

CONSTANZE: Stop it.

MOZART: Stanzy wanzy had a fit. Shit her stays and made them split!

[She giggles despite herself.]

CONSTANZE: Stop it.

MOZART: When they took away her skirt, Stanzy wanzy ate the dirt!

CONSTANZE: Stop it now! [She snatches the ruler and gives him a whack with it. He yowls playfully.]

MOZART: Oooo! Oooo! Oooo! Do it again! Do it again! I cast myself at your stinking feet, Madonna!

[*He does so. She whacks him some more as he crouches, but always lightly, scarcely looking at him, divided between tears and laughter.* MOZART *drums his feet with pleasure.*]

Ow! Ow! Ow!

[*And then suddenly* SALIERI, *unable to bear another second, cries out involuntarily.*]

SALIERI: *Ah!!!*

[*The young couple freezes.* SALIERI, *discovered, hastily converts his noise of disgust into a yawn, and stretches as if waking up from a nap. He peers out of the wing chair.*]

Good evening.

CONSTANZE: [Embarrassed]. Excellency . . .

MOZART: How long have you been there?

SALIERI: I was asleep until a second ago. Are you two quarreling?

MOZART: No, of course not.

CONSTANZE: Yes, we are. He's been very irritating.

SALIERI: [Rising]. *Caro Herr*, tonight is the time for New Year resolutions. Irritating lovely ladies cannot surely be one of yours. May I suggest you bring us each a *sorbetto* from the dining room?

MOZART: But why don't we all go to the table?

CONSTANZE: Herr Salieri is quite right. Bring them here—it'll be your punishment.

MOZART: Stanzi!

SALIERI: Come now, I can keep your wife company. There cannot be a better peace offering than a *sorbetto* of aniseed.

CONSTANZE: I prefer tangerine.

SALIERI: Very well, tangerine. [*Greedily*] But if you could possibly manage aniseed for me, I'd be deeply obliged ... So the New Year can begin coolly for all three of us.

[*A pause.* MOZART *hesitates—and then bows.*]

MOZART: I'm honored, Signore, of course. And then I'll play you at billiards. What do you say?

SALIERI: I'm afraid I don't play.

MOZART: [*With surprise*]. You don't?

CONSTANZE: Wolferl would rather play at billiards than anything. He's very good at it.

MOZART: I'm the best! I may nod occasionally at composing, but at billiards—never!

SALIERI: A virtuoso of the cue.

MOZART: Exactly! It's a virtuoso's game! ... [*He snatches up the ruler and treats it as if it were a cue.*] I think I shall write a Grand Fantasia for Billiard Balls! Trills. Accacciaturas! Whole arpeggios in ivory! Then I'll play it myself in public! ... It'll have to be me because none of those Italian charlatans like

Clementi will be able to get his fingers round the cue! *Scusate, Signore!*

[*He gives a swanky flourish of the hand and struts offstage.*]

CONSTANZE: He's a love, really.

SALIERI: And lucky too, in you. You are, if I may say so, an astonishing creature.

CONSTANZE: Me? . . . Ta very much.

SALIERI: On the other hand, your husband does not appear to be so thriving.

CONSTANZE: [*Seizing her opportunity*]. We're desperate, sir.

SALIERI: What?

CONSTANZE: We've no money and no prospects of any. That's the truth.

SALIERI: I don't understand. He gives many public concerts.

CONSTANZE: They don't pay enough. What he needs is pupils. Illustrious pupils. His father calls us spendthrifts, but that's unfair. I manage as well as anyone could. There's simply not enough. Don't tell him I talked to you, please.

SALIERI: [*Intimately*]. This is solely between us. How can I help?

CONSTANZE: My husband needs security, sir. If only he could find regular employment, everything would be all right. Is there nothing at court?

SALIERI: Not at the moment.

CONSTANZE: [*Harder*]. The Princess Elizabeth needs a tutor.

SALIERI: Really? I hadn't heard.

CONSTANZE: One word from you and the post would be his. Other pupils would follow at once.

SALIERI: [*Looking off*]. He's coming back.

CONSTANZE: Please . . . please, Excellency. You can't imagine what a difference it would make.

SALIERI: We can't speak of it now.

CONSTANZE: When, then? Oh, please!

SALIERI: Can you come and see me tomorrow? Alone?

CONSTANZE: I can't do that.

SALIERI: I'm a married man.

CONSTANZE: All the same.

SALIERI: When does he work?

CONSTANZE: Afternoons.

SALIERI: Then come at three.

CONSTANZE: I can't possibly!

SALIERI: Yes or no? . . . In his interests? . . .

[*A pause. Constanze hesitates—opens her mouth—then smiles and abruptly runs off. The curtains descend on the Light Box.*]

SALIERI: [*To audience*]. So: I'd done it! Spoken aloud! Invited her! . . . What of that vow made in church? Fidelity—virtue—all of that? I couldn't think of that now!

[*SERVANTS remove the Waldstädten furniture. Others replace it with two small gilded*

(*Above*) The old Antonio Salieri (F. MURRAY ABRAHAM), hospitalized after his attempted suicide, tells the story of his struggle with God and with Mozart.

(*Below*) Salieri and his prize pupil, Katherina Cavalieri (CHRISTINE EBERSOLE), during a voice lesson in Salieri's home.

Against his father's wishes, Wolfgang Mozart (TOM HULCE) marries Constanze Weber (ELIZABETH BERRIDGE), his landlady's daughter.

Seeking Salieri's support for an important Imperial post, Mozart brings his music manuscript to Salieri for his opinion.

Mozart dresses as a unicorn for the masquerade ball.

Against a backdrop of fairy tale characters, costumed couples dance during the masquerade ball.

Salieri takes advantage of the Mozarts' absence to visit, uninvited, the composer's workroom and examine his manuscripts.

Count Orsini-Rosenberg (CHARLES KAY), Director of the Imperial Opera, Kapellmeister Giuseppe Bonno (PATRICK HINES), and Salieri at a rehearsal of Mozart's opera *The Marriage of Figaro*.

Mozart conducts *The Marriage of Figaro* as the Emperor Joseph II (JEFFREY JONES) watches from the front row.

Salieri conducting a performance of his opera *Axur* at the Vienna Opera House, before an audience that includes the Emperor Joseph II.

Flanked by three actresses, Mozart passionately applauds the performance of *Axur*.

The Emperor Joseph II honors Salieri with a medal following the performance of *Axur*.

Mozart conducting a performance of *Don Giovanni* at the Vienna Opera House before a half-empty theater.

Salieri disguised as the menacing figure from Mozart's dream.

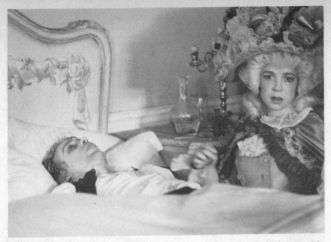

After collapsing during a performance of *The Magic Flute* at the Emmanuel Schikaneder Theatre, Mozart, attended by his wife, Constanze, lies on his deathbed.

The aged, embittered Salieri recovers from his attempted suicide in the General Infirmary of Vienna.

chairs, center, quite close together. Others, again surreptitiously, bring in the old dressing gown and cap which SALIERI discarded before Scene 3, placing them on the forte-piano.]

SCENE 11

Salieri's Apartment

[On the curtains are thrown projections of long windows.]

SALIERI: Next afternoon I waited in a fever. Would she come? I had no idea. And if she did, how would I behave? Was I actually going to seduce a young wife of two months standing? . . . Part of me—much of me—wanted it, badly. *Badly.* Yes, badly was the word!

[The clock strikes three. On the second stroke, the bell sounds. He rises excitedly.]

There she was! On the stroke! She'd come . . . She'd come!

[Enter from the right the COOK, as fat, but forty years younger. He proudly carries a

plate piled with brandied chestnuts. SALIERI takes them from him nervously, nodding with approval, and sets them on the table.]
[To the COOK] Grazie. Grazie tanti. . . . Via, via, via!

[The COOK bows as SALIERI dismisses him, and goes out the same way, smirking suggestively. The VALET comes in from the left—he is also forty years younger—and behind him CONSTANZE, wearing a pretty hat and carrying a portfolio.]

SALIERI: Signora!

CONSTANZE: [Curtsying]. Excellency.

SALIERI: Benvenuta. [To VALET in dismissal] Grazie.

[The VALET goes]
Well. You have come.

CONSTANZE: I should not have done. My husband would be frantic if he knew. He's a very jealous man.

SALIERI: Are you a jealous woman?

CONSTANZE: Why do you ask?

SALIERI: It's not a passion I understand . . . You're looking even prettier than you were last night, if I may say so.

CONSTANZE: Ta very much! . . . I brought you some manuscripts by Wolfgang. When you see them, you'll understand how right he is for a royal appointment. Will you look at them, please, while I wait?

SALIERI: You mean now?

CONSTANZE: Yes, I have to take them back with me. He'll miss them otherwise. He doesn't make copies. These are all the originals.

SALIERI: Sit down. Let me offer you something special.

CONSTANZE: [*Sitting*]. What's that?

SALIERI: [*Producing the box*]. *Capezzoli di Venere*. Nipples of Venus. Roman chestnuts in brandied sugar.

CONSTANZE: No, thank you.

SALIERI: Do try. My cook made them especially for you.

CONSTANZE: Me?

SALIERI: Yes. They're quite rare.

CONSTANZE: Well then, I'd better, hadn't I? Just one ... Ta very much. [*She takes one and puts it in her mouth. The taste amazes her.*] Oh! ... Oh! ... Oh! ... They're *delish*!

SALIERI: [*Lustfully watching her eat*]. Aren't they?

CONSTANZE: Mmmmm!

SALIERI: Have another.

CONSTANZE: [*Taking two more*]. I couldn't possibly.

[*Carefully he moves round behind her, and seats himself on the chair next to her.*]

SALIERI: I think you're the most generous girl in the world.

CONSTANZE: Generous?

SALIERI: It's my word for you. I thought last night that Constanze is altogether too stiff a name for that girl. I shall rechristen her Generosa. *La Generosa.* Then I'll write a glorious song for her under that title and she'll sing it, just for me.

CONSTANZE: [*Smiling*]. I am much out of practice, sir.

SALIERI: *La Generosa.* [*He leans a little toward her.*] Don't tell me it's going to prove inaccurate, my name for you.

CONSTANZE: [*Coolly*]. What name do you give your wife, Excellency?

SALIERI: [*Equally coolly*]. I'm not an excellency, and I call my wife Signora Salieri. If I named her anything else, it would be *La Statua.* She is a very upright lady.

CONSTANZE: Is she here now? I'd like to meet her.

SALIERI: Alas, no. At the moment she's visiting her mother in Verona.

[*She starts very slightly out of her chair. SALIERI gently restrains her.*]

SALIERI: Constanze: tomorrow evening I dine with the Emperor. One word from me recommending your husband as tutor to the Princess Elizabeth, and that invaluable post is his. Believe me, when I speak to His Majesty in matters musical, no one contradicts me.

CONSTANZE: I believe you.

SALIERI: Bene. [*Still sitting, he takes his* mouchoir *and delicately wipes her mouth with it.*] Surely service of that sort deserves a little recompense in return?

CONSTANZE: How little?

[*Slight pause*]

SALIERI: The size of a kiss.

[*Slight pause*]

CONSTANZE: Just one?

[*Slight pause*]

SALIERI: If one seems fair to you.

[*She looks at him—then kisses him lightly on the mouth. Longer pause*]

Does it?

[*She gives him a longer kiss. He makes to touch her with his hand. She breaks off.*]

CONSTANZE: I fancy that's fairness enough.

[*Pause*]

SALIERI: [*Carefully*]. A pity ... It's somewhat small pay, to secure a post every musician in Vienna is hoping for.

CONSTANZE: What do you mean?

SALIERI: Is it not clear?

CONSTANZE: No. Not at all.

SALIERI: Another pity ... A thousand pities.

[*Pause*]

CONSTANZE: I don't believe it ... I just don't believe it!

SALIERI: What?

CONSTANZE: What you've just said.

67

SALIERI: [*Hastily*]. I said nothing. What did I say?

[CONSTANZE *gets up and* SALIERI *rises in panic.*]

CONSTANZE: Oh, I'm going! . . . I'm getting out of this!

SALIERI: Constanze . . .

CONSTANZE: Let me pass, please.

SALIERI: Constanze, listen to me! I'm a clumsy man. You think me sophisticated—I'm not at all. Take a true look. I've no cunning. I live on ink and sweetmeats. I never see women at all. . . . When I met you last night, I envied Mozart from the depths of my soul. Out of that envy came stupid thoughts. For one silly second I dared imagine that, out of the vast store you obviously possess, you might spare me one coin of tenderness your rich husband does not need—and inspire me also.

[*Pause. She laughs.*]

I amuse.

CONSTANZE: Mozart was right. You're wicked.

SALIERI: He said that?

CONSTANZE: "All wops are performers," he said. "Be very careful with that one." Meaning you. He was being comic, of course.

SALIERI: Yes.

[*Abruptly he turns his back on her.*]

CONSTANZE: But not that comic, actually. I mean, you're acting a pretty obvious role, aren't you, dear? A small-town boy, and all the time as clever as cutlets! . . . [*Mock tender*] Ah! You are sulking? Are you? . . . When Mozart sulks, I smack his botty. He rather likes it. Do you want me to scold you a bit and smack your botty too? [*She hits him lightly with the portfolio. He turns in a fury.*]

SALIERI: How dare you?! . . . You silly, common girl!

[*A dreadful silence*]

[*Icy*] Forgive me. Let us confine our talk to your husband. He is a brilliant keyboard player, no question. However, the Princess Elizabeth also requires a tutor in vocal music. I am not convinced he is the man for that. I would like to look at the pieces you've brought, and decide if he is mature enough. I will study them overnight—and you will study my proposal. Not to be vague, that is the price. [*He extends his hand for the portfolio, and she surrenders it.*] Good afternoon.

[*He turns from her and places it on a chair. She lingers—tries to speak—cannot—and goes out quickly.*]

SCENE 12

The Same

[SALIERI *turns in a ferment to the audience.*]

SALIERI: Fiasco! . . . Fiasco! . . . The sordidness of it! The sheer sweating sordidness! . . . Worse than if I'd actually done it! . . . To be that much in sin and feel so *ridiculous* as well! [*Crying out*] Nobile, nobile Salieri! . . . What had he done to me, this Mozart? Before he came, did I behave like this? Did I? Toy with adultery? Blackmail women? It was all going—slipping—growing rotten . . . because of him!

[*He moves upstage in a fever—reaches out to take the portfolio on the chair—but as if fearful of what he might find inside it, he withdraws his hand and sits instead. A pause. He contemplates the music lying there as if it were a great confection he is dying to eat, but dare not. Then suddenly he snatches at it—tears the ribbon—opens*

70

*the case and stares greedily at the manu-
scripts within.*

*Music sounds instantly, faintly, in the
theater, as his eye falls on the first page.
It is the opening of the Twenty-ninth
Symphony, in A major. Over the music,
reading it.]*

She had said that these were his original
scores. First and only drafts of the music. Yet
they looked like fair copies. They showed no
corrections of any kind. It was puzzling—then
suddenly alarming.

*[He looks up from the manuscript at the
audience: the music abruptly stops.]*

What was evident was that Mozart was simply transcribing music completely finished
in his head. And finished as most music is
never finished.

*[He resumes looking at the music. Immedi-
ately the Sinfonia Concertante for Violin
and Viola sounds.]*

Displace one note and there would be dimin-
ishment. Displace one phrase and the struc-
ture would fall.

[He looks up again: the music breaks off.]

Here again—only now in abundance—were
the same sounds I'd heard in the library.

*[He resumes reading, and the music also
resumes: a ravishing phrase from the slow*

movement of the Concerto for Flute and Harp.]

The same crushed harmonies—glancing collisions—agonizing delights.

[He looks up again. The music stops.]

The truth was clear. That Serenade had been no accident.

[Very low, in the theater, a faint thundery sound is heard accumulating, like a distant sea.]

I was staring through the cage of those meticulous ink strokes at—an Absolute Beauty!

[And out of the thundery roar writhes and rises the clear sound of a soprano, singing the Kyrie from the C Minor Mass. The accretion of noise around her voice falls away—it is suddenly clear and bright—then clearer and brighter. The light grows bright: too bright: burning white, then scalding white! SALIERI rises in the downpour of it, and in the flood of the music, which is growing ever louder—filling the theater—as the soprano yields to the full chorus, fortissimo, singing its massive counterpoint. This is by far the loudest sound the audience has yet heard. SALIERI staggers toward us, holding the manuscripts in his hand, like a man caught in a tumbling and violent sea. Finally the drums crash in below: SALIERI drops the portfolio of manuscripts—

and falls senseless to the ground. At the same second the music explodes into a long, echoing, distorted boom, signifying some dreadful annihilation.

The sound remains suspended over the prone figure in a menacing continuum—no longer music at all. Then it dies away, and there is only silence.

The light fades again.

A long pause.

SALIERI is quite still, his head by the pile of manuscripts. Finally the clock sounds: nine times. SALIERI stirs as it does. Slowly he raises his head and looks up. And now— quietly at first—he addresses his God.]

SALIERI: Capisco! I know my fate. Now for the first time I feel my emptiness as Adam felt his nakedness. . . . [Slowly he rises to his feet.] Tonight at an inn somewhere in this city stands a giggling child who can put on paper, without actually setting down his billiard cue, casual notes which turn my most considered ones into lifeless scratches. Grazie, Signore! You gave me the desire to serve You—which most men do not have—then saw to it the service was shameful in the ears of the server. Grazie! You gave me the desire to praise You—which most men do not feel—then made me mute. Grazie tanti! You put into me perception of the Incomparable—which

73

most men never know!—then ensured that I
would know myself forever mediocre. [*His
voice gains power.*] *Why?* ... *What is my
fault?* ... Until this day I have pursued virtue with rigor. I have labored long hours to
relieve my fellow men. I have worked and
worked the talent You allowed me. [*Calling
up*] *You know how hard I've worked!* Solely
that in the end, in the practice of the art
which alone makes the world comprehensible to me, I might hear Your Voice! And now
I do hear it—and it says only one name:
MOZART! ... Spiteful, sniggering, conceited,
infantine Mozart—who has never worked one
minute to help another man! Shit-talking
Mozart, with his botty-smacking wife! *Him*
You have chosen to be Your sole conduct!
And *my* only reward—my sublime privilege—
is to be the sole man alive in this time who
shall clearly recognize Your Incarnation!
[*Savagely*] *Grazie e grazie ancora!* [*Pause*]
So be it! From this time we are enemies, You
and I! I'll not accept it from You—*do you
hear?* ... They say God is not mocked. I tell
You, *Man* is not mocked! ... *I* am not mocked!
... They say the spirit bloweth where it listeth:
I tell You NO! It must list to virtue or not
blow at all! [*Yelling*] *Dio ingiusto*—You are
the Enemy! I name Thee now—*Nemico Eterno!*
And this I swear: To my last breath I shall

block. You on earth, as far as I am able! [*He glares up at God. To audience*] What use, after all, is man, if not to teach God His lessons? [*Pause. Suddenly he speaks again to us in the voice of an old man. He slips off his powdered wig, crosses to the fortepiano and takes from its lid where they lie the old dressing gown and cap which he discarded when he conducted us back to the eighteenth century. He slips these on. It is again 1823.*] Before I tell you what happened next—God's answer to me—and indeed Constanze's—and all the horrors that followed—let me stop. The bladder, being a human appendage, is not something you need concern yourselves with yet. I, being alive, though barely, am at its constant call. It is now one hour before dawn—when I must dismiss us both. When I return, I'll tell you about the war I fought with God through His preferred Creature—Mozart, named *Amadeus.* In the waging of which, of course, the Creature had to be destroyed.

[*He bows to the audience with malignant slyness—snatches a pastry from the stand— and leaves the stage, chewing at it voraciously. The manuscripts lie where he spilled them in his fall. The lights in the theater come up as he goes.*]

END OF ACT ONE

ACT TWO

SCENE 1

Salieri's Apartment

[*The lights go down in the theater as* SALIERI *returns.*]

SALIERI: I have been listening to the cats in the courtyard. They are all singing Rossini. It is obvious that cats have declined as badly as composers. Domenico Scarlatti owned one which would actually stroll across the keyboard and pick out passable subjects for fugue. But that was a Spanish cat of the Enlightenment. It appreciated counterpoint. Nowadays all cats appreciate is coloratura. Like the rest of the public.

[*He comes downstage and addresses the audience directly.*]

This is now the very last hour of my life. You must understand me. Not forgive. I do not seek forgiveness. I was a good man, as the world calls good. What use was it to me? Goodness could not make me a good composer! ... Was Mozart good? Goodness is nothing in the furnace of art.

[*Pause*]

On that dreadful Night of the Manuscripts my life acquired a terrible and thrilling purpose. The blocking of God in one of His purest manifestations. I had the power. God needed Mozart to let Himself into the world. And Mozart needed me to get him worldly advancement. So it would be a battle to the end—and Mozart was the battleground.

[*Pause*]

One thing I knew of Him. He was a cunning Enemy. Witness the fact that in blocking Him in the world I was also given the satisfaction of obstructing a disliked human rival. I wonder which of you will refuse that chance if it is offered.

[*He regards the audience maliciously and takes off the dressing gown and cap.*]

I felt the danger at once, as soon as I'd spoken my challenge. How would He answer? Would He strike me dead for my impiety? Don't laugh. I was not a sophisticate of the salons. I was a small-town Catholic, full of dread!

[*He puts on the powdered wig again and speaks again in his younger voice. We are back again in the eighteenth century.*]

The first thing that happened, barely one hour later—

[*The doorbell sounds.* CONSTANZE *comes in, followed by a helpless* VALET.]

Suddenly Constanze was back. At ten o'clock at night.

[*In surprise*]

Signora!

CONSTANZE: [*Stiffly*]. My husband is at a soiree of Baron van Swieten. A concert of Sebastian Bach. He didn't think I would enjoy it.

SALIERI: I see. [*Curtly, to the goggling* VALET] I'll ring if we require anything. Thank you.

[*The* VALET *goes out. Slight pause.*]

CONSTANZE: [*Flatly*]. Where do we go, then?

SALIERI: What?

CONSTANZE: Do we do it in here? . . . Why not?

[*She sits, still wearing her hat, in one of the little gilded upright chairs. Deliberately she loosens the strings of her bodice, so that one can just see the tops of her breasts, hitches up her silk skirts above the knees, so that one can also just see the flesh above the tops of the stockings, spreads her legs and regards him with an open stare.*]

[*Speaking softly*] Well? . . . Let's get on with it.

[*For a second* SALIERI *returns the stare, then looks suddenly away.*]

SALIERI: [*Stiffly*]. Your manuscripts are there. Please take them and go. Now. At once.

[*Pause*]

CONSTANZE: You shit. [*She jumps up and snatches the portfolio.*]

SALIERI: *Via! Don't return!*

CONSTANZE: You rotten shit!

[*Suddenly she runs at him, trying furiously to hit at his face. He grabs her arms, shakes her violently, and hurls her on the floor.*]

SALIERI: *Via!*

[*She freezes, staring up at him in hate.*]

[*Calling to audience*] You see how it was! I would have liked her—oh, yes, just then more than ever! I wanted nothing petty! . . . My quarrel now wasn't with Mozart—it was through him! Through him to God, who loved him so. [*Scornfully*] Amadeus! . . . Amadeus! . . .

[CONSTANZE *picks herself up and runs from the room. Pause. He calms himself, going to the table and selecting a "Nipple of Venus" to eat.*]

The next day, when Katherina Cavalieri came for her lesson, I made the same halting speech about "coins of tenderness," and I dubbed the girl *La Generosa*. I regret that my invention in love, as in art, has always been limited. Fortunately, Katherina found it sufficient. She consumed twenty "Nipples of Venus"—kissed me with brandied breath—and slipped easily into my bed.

[KATHERINA *comes in languidly, half undressed, as if from his bedroom. He embraces her, and helps slyly to adjust her peignoir.*]

She remained there as my mistress for many years behind my good wife's back—and I soon erased in sweat the sense of his little body, the Creature's, preceding me.

[*The girl gives him a radiant smile, and ambles off.*]

So much for my vow of sexual virtue. [*Slight pause*] The same evening I went to the Palace and resigned from all my committees to help the lot of poor musicians. So much for my vow of social virtue.

[*Light change*]

Then I went to the Emperor and recommended a man of no talent whatever to instruct the Princess Elizabeth.

81

SCENE 2

The Palace of Schönbrunn

[The EMPEROR *stands before the vast fire-place, between the golden mirrors.*]

JOSEPH: Herr Sommer. A dull man, surely? What of Mozart?

SALIERI: Majesty, I cannot with a clear conscience recommend Mozart to teach royalty. One hears too many stories.

JOSEPH: They may be just gossip.

SALIERI: One of them, I regret, relates to a protégée of my own. A very young singer.

JOSEPH: *Charmant!*

SALIERI: Not pleasant, Majesty, but true.

JOSEPH: I see ... Let it be Herr Sommer, then. [*He walks down onto the main stage.*] I daresay he can't do much harm. To be frank, no one can do much harm musically to the Princess Elizabeth. [*He strolls away.*]

[MOZART *enters from the other side, downstage. He wears a more natural-looking wig*

from now on—one indeed intended to represent his own hair of light chestnut, full
and gathered at the back with ribbon.]

SALIERI: [To audience]. Mozart certainly did not
suspect me. The Emperor announced the appointment in his usual way—

JOSEPH: [Pausing]. Well—there it is. [He goes off.]

SALIERI: And I commiserated with the loser.

[MOZART turns and stares bleakly out front.
SALIERI shakes his hand.]

MOZART: [Bitterly]. It's my own fault. My father
always writes I should be more obedient.
Know my place! . . . He'll send me sixteen
lectures when he hears of this!

[MOZART goes slowly up to the fortepiano.
Lights lower.]

SALIERI: [Watching him, to audience]. It was a
most serious loss as far as Mozart was concerned.

SCENE 3

Vienna, and Glimpses of Opera Houses

[The VENTICELLI glide on.]

V.1: His list of pupils hardly moves.

V.2: Six at most.

V.1: And now a child to keep!

V.2: A boy.

SALIERI: Poor fellow. [*To audience*] I by contrast prospered. This is the extraordinary truth. If I had expected fury from God, none came. None! . . . Instead—incredibly—in '84 and '85 I came to be regarded as infinitely the superior composer. And this despite the fact that these were the two years in which Mozart wrote his best keyboard concerti and his string quartets.

[The VENTICELLI stand on either side of SALIERI. MOZART sits at the fortepiano.]

V.1: Haydn calls the quartets unsurpassed.

SALIERI: They were, but no one heard them.

V.2: Van Swieten calls the concerti sublime.

SALIERI: They were, but no one noticed.

[MOZART *plays and conducts from the keyboard. Faintly we heard the Rondo from the Piano Concert in A major, K. 488.*]

[*Over this*] The Viennese greeted each concerto with the squeals of pleasure they usually reserved for a new style of bonnet. Each was played once—then totally forgotten! ... By contrast, my operas were played everywhere and saluted by everyone! I composed a *Semiramide* for Munich.

V.1: Rapturously received!

V.2: People *faint* with pleasure!

[*In the Light Box is seen the interior of a brilliantly colored opera house, and an audience standing up, applauding vigorously. SALIERI, flanked by the VENTICELLI, turns upstage and bows to it. The concerts can barely be heard through the din.*]

SALIERI: I wrote a comic opera for Vienna. *La Grotta di Trofonio.*

V.1: The talk of the city!

V.2: The cafés are buzzing!

[*Another opera house interior is lit up. Another audience claps vigorously. Again SALIERI bows to it.*]

SALIERI: [*To audience*]. I finally finished my tragic opera *Danaius*, and produced in it Paris.

V.1: Stupendous reception!

V.2: The plaudits shake the roof!

V.1: Your name sounds throughout the Empire!
V.2: Throughout all Europe!
[*Yet another opera house and another ex-cited audience.* SALIERI *bows a third time. Even the* VENTICELLI *now applaude him. The concert stops.* MOZART *rises from the keyboard and, while* SALIERI *speaks, crosses directly through the scene and leaves the stage.*]
SALIERI: [*To audience*]. It was incomprehensible. Almost as if I were being pushed deliberately from triumph to triumph! . . . I filled my head with golden opinions—yes, and this house with golden furniture!

SCENE 4

Salieri's Apartment

[*The stage turns gold.*
SERVANTS *come on carrying golden chairs upholstered in golden brocade. They place these all over the wooden floor. The* VALET *appears—a little older—divests* SALIERI *of*

his sky-blue coat and clothes him instead in a frock coat of gold satin.

The COOK—*also, of course, a little older—brings in a golden cake-stand piled with more elaborate cakes.*]

SALIERI: My own taste was for plain things—but I denied it! The successful lived with gold, and so would I! ... I grew confident. I grew resplendent. I gave salons and soirees, and worshiped the season round at the altar of sophistication!

[*He sits at ease in his salon. The* VENTICELLI *sit with him, one on either side.*]

V.1: Mozart heard your comedy last night.

V.2: He spoke of it to the Princess Lichnowsky.

V.1: He said you should be made to clean up your own mess.

SALIERI: [*Taking snuff*]. *Really?* What charmers these Salzburgers are!

V.2: People are outraged by him.

V.1: He empties drawing rooms. Now Van Swieten is angry with him.

[*The* VENTICELLI *laugh maliciously.*]

SALIERI: Lord Fugue? ... I thought he was the Baron's little pet.

V.2: Mozart has asked leave to write an Italian opera.

SALIERI: [*To audience*]. *Italian opera! Threat! My kingdom!*

V.1: And the Baron is scandalized.

SALIERI: But why? What's the subject?

    [VAN SWIETEN *comes on quickly from up-*
    stage.]

VAN SWIETEN: Figaro! . . . The Marriage of Figaro!
That disgraceful play of Beaumarchais!

    [*At a discreet sign of dismissal from* SALIERI,
    the VENTICELLI *slip away.* VAN SWIETEN *joins*
    SALIERI, *and sits on one of the gold chairs.*]

VAN SWIETEN: [*To* SALIERI]. That's all he can
find to waste his talent on: a vulgar farce!
Noblemen lusting after chambermaids! Their
wives dressing up in stupid diguises anyone
could penetrate in a second! . . . When I re-
proved him, he said I reminded him of his
father! . . . I simply cannot imagine why Mozart should want to set that rubbish to music!

    [MOZART *enters quickly from upstage, ac-*
    companied by STRACK. *They join* SALIERI
    and VAN SWIETEN.]

MOZART: Because I want to do a piece about
real people, Baron! And I want to set it in a
real place! A *boudoir!* Because that to me is
the most exciting place on earth! Underclothes
on the floor! Sheets still warm from a woman's
body! Even a pisspot brimming under the
bed!

VAN SWIETEN: [*Outraged*]. Mozart!

MOZART: I want life, Baron. Not boring legends!

STRACK: Herr Salieri's recent *Danaius* was a
legend, and that did not bore the French.

MOZART: It is impossible to bore the French—except with real life!

VAN SWIETEN: I had assumed, now that you had joined our Brotherhood of Masons, you would choose more elevated themes.

MOZART: [Impatiently]. Oh, elevated! Elevated! ... The only thing a man should elevate is his doodle.

VAN SWIETEN: You are provoking, sir! Has everything to be a joke with you?

MOZART: [Desperate]. Excuse the language, Baron, but really! ... How can we go on forever with these gods and heroes?

VAN SWIETEN: [Passionately]. Because they go on forever—that's why! They represent the eternal in us. Opera is here to ennoble us, Mozart—you and me just as well as the Emperor. It is an aggrandizing art! It celebrates the eternal in man and ignores the ephemeral. The goddess in woman and not the laundress.

STRACK: Well said, sir. Exactly!

MOZART: [Imitating his drawl]. Oh, well said, yes, well said! Exactly! [To all of them] I don't understand you! You're all up on perches, but it doesn't hide your arseholes! You don't give a shit about gods and heroes! If you are honest—each one of you—which of you isn't more at home with his hairdresser than Hercules? Or Horatius?

[To SALIERI] Or your stupid Danaius, come to that! Or mine—mine! *Idomeneo, King of Crete!* All those anguished antiques! They're all bores! Bores, bores, bores! [*Suddenly he springs up and jumps onto a chair, like an orator. Declaring it*] All serious operas written this century are boring!

[*They turn and look at him in shocked amazement. A pause. He gives his little giggle, and then jumps down again.*]

Look at us! Four gaping mouths. What a perfect quartet! I'd love to write it—just this second of time, this *now*, as you are! Herr Chamberlain thinking: "Impertinent Mozart. I must speak to the Emperor at once!" Herr Prefect thinking: "Ignorant Mozart. Debasing opera with his vulgarity!" Herr Court Composer thinking: "German Mozart. What can he finally know about music?" And Mozart himself, in the middle, thinking: "I'm just a good fellow. Why do they all disapprove of me?" [*Excitedly to* VAN SWIETEN] That's why opera is important, Baron. Because it's realer than any play! A dramatic poet would have to put all those thoughts down one after another to represent this second of time. The composer can put them all down at once— and still make us hear each one of them. Astonishing device—a vocal quartet! [*More and more excited*] I tell you I want to write a finale lasting half an hour! A quartet becoming a quintet becoming a sextet. On and on, wider and wider—all sounds multiplying and rising together—and then together making a sound entirely new! ... I bet you that's how God hears the world. Millions of sounds ascending at once and mixing in His ear to become an unending music, unimaginable to us! [To SALIERI] That's our job! That's our job, we composers: to combine the inner minds of him and him and him, and her and her—the thoughts of chambermaids and Court Composers—and turn the audience into God.

[Pause. SALIERI stares at him, fascinated. Embarrassed, MOZART sounds a fart noise and giggles.]

I'm sorry. I talk nonsense all day. It's incurable—ask Stanzerl.

[To VAN SWIETEN] My tongue is stupid. My heart isn't.

VAN SWIETEN: No. You're a good fellow under all your nonsense: I know that. He'll make a fine new Brother, won't he, Salieri?

SALIERI: Better than I, Baron.

VAN SWIETEN: Just try, my friend, to be more serious with your gifts.

[He smiles, presses MOZART's hand, and goes. SALIERI rises.]

SALIERI: Buona fortuna, Mozart.

MOZART: Grazie, Signore. [Rounding on STRACK]

Stop frowning, Herr Chamberlain. I'm a jackass. It's easy to be friends with a jackass: just
shake his hoof.

> [*He forms his hand into a hoof. Warily*
> STRACK *takes it—then springs back as* MO-
> ZART *brays loudly like a donkey.*]

Hee-haw! . . . Tell the Emperor the opera's
finished.

STRACK: Finished?

MOZART: Right here in my noodle. The rest's
just scribbling. Goodbye.

STRACK: Good day to you.

MOZART: He's going to be proud of me. You'll
see! [*He gives his flourish of the hand and
goes out, delighted with himself.*]

STRACK: That young man *really is* . . .

SALIERI: [*Blandly*]. Very lively!

STRACK: [*Exploding*]. Intolerable! . . . *Intolerable!*
[STRACK *freezes in a posture of indignation.*]

SALIERI: [*To audience*]. How could I stop it? . . .
How could I block this opera of Figaro? . . .
Incredible to hear, within six weeks the Crea-
ture had finished the entire score!

> [ROSENBERG *bustles in.*]

ROSENBERG: Figaro is complete! The first performance will be on May the first.

SALIERI: So soon?

ROSENBERG: There's no way we can stop it! [*A
slight pause*]

SALIERI: [*Slyly*]. I have an idea. *Una piccola idea.*

ROSENBERG: What?

SALIERI: *Mi ha detto che c'è un balletto nel terzo atto?*

ROSENBERG: [Puzzled]. *Sì.*

STRACK: What does he say?

SALIERI: *E dimmi—non è vero che l'Imperatore ha proibito il balletto nelle sue opere?*

ROSENBERG: [Realizing]. *Uno balletto . . . Ah!*

SALIERI: *Precisamente.*

ROSENBERG: *Oh, capisco! Ma che meraviglia! Perfetto!* [He laughs in delight.] *Veramente ingegnoso!*

STRACK: [Irritated]. What is it? What is he suggesting?

SALIERI: See him at the theater.

ROSENBERG: Of course. Immediately. I'd forgotten. You are brilliant, Court Composer.

SALIERI: I? . . . I have said nothing. [He moves away upstage.]   [The light begins to change, dimming down.]

STRACK: [Very cross]. I must tell you that I resent this extremely. Mozart is right in some things. There is far too much Italian *chittero-chattero* at this court! Now please to inform me at once, what was just said?

ROSENBERG: [Lightly]. *Pazienza,* my dear Chamberlain. *Pazienza.* Just wait and see!

[From upstage, SALIERI beckons to STRACK. Baffled and cross, the CHAMBERLAIN joins him. They watch together, unseen. The light dims further.]

SCENE 5

An Unlit Theater

[In the background, a projection of lamps glowing faintly in the darkened auditorium. ROSENBERG sits on one of the gold chairs, center. MOZART comes in quickly from the left, wearing another bright coat, and carrying the score of Figaro. He crosses to the fortepiano.]

ROSENBERG: Mozart! . . . Mozart!

MOZART: Yes, Herr Director.

ROSENBERG: [Agreeably]. A word with you, please. Right away.

MOZART: Certainly. What is it?

ROSENBERG: I would like to see your score of Figaro.

MOZART: Oh, yes. Why?

ROSENBERG: Just bring it here to me. [Unmoving] Into my hand, please.

[MOZART hands it to him, puzzled. ROSENBERG turns the pages.]

Now tell me: did you know that His Majesty has expressly forbidden ballet in his operas?

MOZART: Ballet?

ROSENBERG: Such as occurs in your third act.

MOZART: That is not a ballet, Herr Director. That is a dance at Figaro's wedding.

ROSENBERG: Exactly. A dance.

MOZART: [*Trying to control himself*]. But the Emperor doesn't mean to prohibit dancing when it's part of the story. He made that law to prevent insertions of stupid ballet like in French operas, and quite right too.

ROSENBERG: [*Raising his voice*]. It is not for you, Herr Mozart, to interpret the Emperor's edicts. Merely to obey them. [*He seizes the offending pages between his fingers.*]

MOZART: What are you doing? ... What are you doing, Excellency?

ROSENBERG: Taking out what should never have been put in.

[*In a terrible silence,* ROSENBERG *tears out the pages.* MOZART *watches in disbelief. Upstage,* SALIERI *and* STRACK *look on together from the dimness.*]

Now, sir, perhaps in future you will obey imperial commands. [*He tears out some more pages.*]

MOZART: But ... But if all that goes—there'll be a hole right at the climax of the story ...

[*Crying out suddenly*] Salieri! This is Salieri's idea!

ROSENBERG: Don't be absurd.

SALIERI: [*To audience*]. How did he think of that?! Nothing I had ever done could possibly make him think of that on his own. Had God given him the idea?!

MOZART: It's a conspiracy. I can smell it. I can smell it! It's a conspiracy!

ROSENBERG: Control yourself!

MOZART: [*Howling*]. But what do you expect me to do? The first performance is two days off!

ROSENBERG: Write it over. That's your forte, is it not?—writing at speed.

MOZART: Not when the music's *perfect*! Not when it's absolutely perfect as it is! ... [*Wildly*] I shall appeal to the Emperor! I'll go to him myself! I'll hold a rehearsal especially for him.

ROSENBERG: The Emperor does not attend rehearsals.

MOZART: He'll attend this one. Make no mistake—he'll come to this one! Then he'll deal with you!

ROSENBERG: This issue is simple. Write your act again today—or withdraw the opera. That's final.

[*Pause. He hands back the mutilated score to its composer.* MOZART *is shaking.*]

MOZART: You shit-pot.

[ROSENBERG turns and walks imperturbably away from him.]

Woppy, foppy, wet-arsed, Italian-loving, shit-pot!

[Serenely, ROSENBERG leaves the stage.]

MOZART: [Screeching after him]. Count Orsini-Rosenberg! ... Rosencunt! ... Rosenbugger! ... I'll hold a rehearsal! You'll see! The Emperor will come! You'll see! You'll see! ... You'll see!! [He throws down his score in a storm of hysterical rage.]

[Upstage in the dimness, STRACK goes out, and SALIERI ventures down toward the shrieking little man. MOZART suddenly becomes aware of him. He turns, his hand shooting out in an involuntary gesture of accusation.]

[To SALIERI] I am forbidden! ... I am— But of course you know already.

SALIERI: [Quietly]. Know what?

[MOZART flings away from him.]

MOZART: [Bitterly]. No matter! [He makes to go.]

SALIERI: [Always blandly]. Mozart, permit me. If you wish, I will speak to the Emperor myself. Ask him to attend a rehearsal.

MOZART: [Amazed]. You wouldn't!

SALIERI: I cannot promise he will come, but I can try.

MOZART: [Returning]. Sir! . . .

SALIERI: Good day. [He puts up his hands, barring further intimacy.]

[MOZART retreats to the fortepiano.]

[To audience] Needless to say, I did nothing whatever in the matter. Yet—to my total stupefaction—

[STRACK and ROSENBERG hurry on downstage.]

In the middle of the last rehearsal of Figaro next day . . .

[The EMPEROR JOSEPH comes on from upstage.]

JOSEPH: [Cheerfully]. Fêtes and fireworks! Fêtes and fireworks! Gentlemen, good afternoon!

SCENE 6

The Theater

SALIERI: [To audience]. Entirely against his usual practice, the Emperor appeared!

[STRACK and ROSENBERG look at each other in consternation. JOSEPH seats himself ex-

citedly on one of the gold chairs, facing
out front. As with the premiere of Seraglio
seen in Act I, he watches the audience as
if it were the opera.]

JOSEPH: I can't wait for this, Mozart, I assure
you! *Je prévois des merveilles!*

MOZART: [*Bowing fervently*]. Majesty!
[*The courtiers sit also:* STRACK *on his right-
hand side,* ROSENBERG *on his left.* SALIERI
also sits, near the keyboard.]

SALIERI: [*To audience*]. What did this mean?
Was this proof God had finally decided to
defend Mozart against me? Was He engaging
with me at last?
[MOZART *passes behind* SALIERI.]

MOZART: [*Earnestly, sotto voce*]. I am so grateful to you, I cannot express—

SALIERI: [*Aside, to him*]. Hush. Say nothing.
[MOZART *goes on quickly to the fortepiano
and sits at it.*]

[*To audience*] One thing about the event
seemed more than coincidence.
[*Music sounds faintly: the end of the third
act of* Figaro, *just before the dance music
starts.*]

Strangely, His Majesty had arrived at precisely the moment when the dancers would
have begun, had not they and their music
been entirely cut.
[*The music stops abruptly.*]

99

He and all of us watched the action proceed in total silence.

[*Flanked by his* COURTIERS, *the* EMPEROR *stares out front, following with his eyes what is obviously a silent pantomime. His face expresses bewilderment.* ROSENBERG *watches his sovereign anxiously. Finally the monarch speaks.*]

JOSEPH: I don't understand. Is it modern?

MOZART: [*Jumping up nervously from the keyboard*]. No, Majesty.

JOSEPH: Then what?

MOZART: The Herr Director has removed a dance that would have occurred at this point.

JOSEPH: [*To* ROSENBERG]. Why was this done?

ROSENBERG: It's your own regulation, Sire. No ballet in your opera.

MOZART: [*Nervously*]. Majesty, this is not a ballet! . . . It is part of a wedding feast—entirely necessary for the story.

JOSEPH: Well, it certainly looks very odd the way it is. I can't say I like it.

MOZART: Nor do I, Majesty.

JOSEPH: Do you like it, Rosenberg?

ROSENBERG: It's not a question of liking, Majesty. Your own law decrees it.

JOSEPH: Yes. All the same, this is nonsense. Look at them: they're like waxworks up there.

ROSENBERG: Well, not exactly, Majesty.

JOSEPH: I don't like waxworks.

MOZART: Nor do I, Majesty.

JOSEPH: Well, who would? What do you say, Salieri?

SALIERI: Italians are fond of waxworks, Majesty. [*Pause*] Our religion is largely based upon them.

JOSEPH: You are *cattivo* again, Court Composer.

STRACK: [*Intervening creamily*]. Your Majesty, Count Rosenberg is very worried that if this music is put back, it will create the most unfortunate precedent. One will have thereafter to endure hours of dancing in opera.

JOSEPH: I think we can guard against that, you know, Chamberlain. I really think we can guard against hours of dancing. [*To* ROSENBERG] Please restore Herr Mozart's music.

ROSENBERG: But, Majesty, I must insist—

JOSEPH: [*With command*]. You will oblige me, Rosenberg! . . . I wish to hear Mozart's music. Do you understand me?

ROSENBERG: Yes, Majesty.

[MOZART *explodes with joy, jumps over a chair and throws himself at* JOSEPH's *feet.*]

MOZART: Oh, God, I thank your Majesty! [*He kisses the* EMPEROR's *hand extravagantly, as at their first meeting.*] Oh, thank you—thank you—thank you, Sire, forever!

JOSEPH: [*Withdrawing hand*]. Yes, yes—very good. A little less enthusiasm, I beg you.
MOZART: [*Abashed*]. Excuse me.
[*The* EMPEROR *rises. All follow suit.*]
JOSEPH: Well—there it is!

SCENE 7

The First Performance of
Figaro

[*The theater glows with light for the first performance of* Figaro. COURTIERS *and* CITIZENS *come in swiftly.*
The EMPEROR *and his* COURT *resume their seats and the others quickly take theirs. In the front row we note* KATHERINA CAVALIERI, *all plumes and sequins, and* KAPELLMEISTER BONNO—*older than ever. Behind them sit* CONSTANZE *and the* VENTICELLI. *All of them stare out at the audience as if we were the opera they have come to see: people of fashion down front; poorer people crowded into the Light Box, upstage.*

SALIERI crosses as he speaks, to where two chairs have been placed side by side apart from the rest, on the left, to form his box. On the chair upstage sits his good wife, TERESA—more statuesque than ever.]

SALIERI: [To audience]. And so Figaro was produced in spite of all my efforts. I sat in my box on May the first, 1786, and watched it happen. A conspicuous defeat for me. And yet I was strangely excited.

[Faintly we hear Figaro singing the tune of "Non più andrai." The stage audience is obviously delighted: they smile out front as they watch the (invisible) action.]

My march! My poor March of Welcome—now set to enchant the world forever!

[It fades. Applause. The EMPEROR rises, and with him the audience, to denote an intermission. JOSEPH greets KATHERINA and BONNO. ROSENBERG and STRACK go to SALIERI's box.]

ROSENBERG: [To Salieri]. Almost in your style, that last bit. But more vulgar, of course. Far more obvious than you would ever be.

STRACK: [Drawling]. Exactly!

[A bell rings for the end of the intermission. The EMPEROR returns quickly to his seat. The audience sits. A pause. All look out front, unmoving.]

SALIERI: [Raptly and quietly, to audience].

Trembling, I heard the second act. [*Pause*]
The restored third act. [*Pause*] The astounding
fourth. What shall I say to you who will one
day hear this last act for yourselves? You
will—because whatever else shall pass away,
this must remain.

[*Faintly we hear the solemn closing ensemble from Act 4 of* Figaro, "Ah! Tutti contenti. Saremo così."*]

[*Over this*] The scene was night in a summer
garden. Pinprick stars gleamed down on shaking summerhouses. Plotters glided behind
pasteboard hedges. I saw a woman, dressed
in her maid's clothes, heard her husband utter
the first tender words he has offered her in
years, only because he thinks she is someone
else. Could one catch a realer moment? And
how, except in a net of pure artifice? The
disguises of opera had been invented for
Mozart. [*He can barely look out at the "stage."*]
The final reconciliation melted sight. [*Pause*]
Through my tears I saw the Emperor . . . yawn.

[JOSEPH *yawns. The music fades. There is
scant applause.* JOSEPH *rises and the* COURTIERS *follow suit.* MOZART *bows.*]

JOSEPH [*To* ROSENBERG]: [*Coolly*]. Most ingenious,
Mozart. You are coming along nicely. . . . I do
think we must omit encores in future. It
really makes things far too long. Make a note,
Rosenberg.

ROSENBERG: Majesty.

[MOZART *lowers his head, crushed.*]

JOSEPH: Gentlemen, good night to you. Strack, attend me.

[JOSEPH *goes out, with* STRACK. *Director* ROSENBERG *gives* MOZART *one triumphant look and follows.* SALIERI *nods to his* WIFE, *who leaves with the audience. Only* CONSTANZE *lingers for a second, then she, too, goes. A pause.* MOZART *and* SALIERI *are left alone,* SALIERI *deeply shaken by the opera,* MOZART *deeply upset by its reception. He sits.*]

MOZART: [*Low*]. Herr Salieri.

SALIERI: Yes?

MOZART: What do you think? Do you think I am coming along nicely?

[*A pause*]

SALIERI: [*Moved*]. I think the piece is . . . extraordinary. I think it is . . . marvelous. Yes.

[*A pause*]

MOZART: I'll tell you what it is. It's the best opera yet written. That's what it is. And only I could have done it. No one else living!

[MOZART *walks away.* SALIERI *turns his head away swiftly, as if he has been slapped. They both freeze. The light changes. The* VENTICELLI *rush on.*]

V.1: Rosenberg is furious.

V.2: He'll never forgive Mozart.

V.1: He'll do anything to get back at him!

SALIERI: [Rising, to audience]. So it wasn't hard to get the piece canceled. I saw to it through the person of the resentful Director that in the entire year, Figaro was played only nine times! ... My defeat finally turned into a victory. And God's response to my challenge remained as inscrutable as ever. ... Was He taking any notice of me at all? ...

[MOZART breaks his freeze and comes downstage.]

MOZART: Withdrawn! Absolutely no plans for its revival!

SALIERI: I commiserate with you, my friend. But if the public does not like one's work, one has to accept the fact gracefully.

[Aside, to audience] And certainly they didn't.

V.1: [Complaining]. It's too complicated!

V.2: [Complaining]. Too tiresome!

V.1: All those morbid harmonies!

V.2: And never a good bang at the end of songs, so you know when to clap!

[The VENTICELLI go off.]

SALIERI: [To audience]. Obviously I would not need to plot too hard against his operas in future. I must concentrate on the man. I decided to see him as much as possible: to learn everything I could of his weaknesses.

SCENE 8

The Waldstädten Library

[SERVANTS *again bring on the wing chair.*]

MOZART: I'll go to England! England loves music. That's the answer!

SALIERI: [*To audience*]. We were yet again in the library of the Baroness Waldstädten—that room fated to be the scene of ghastly encounters between us. Again, too, the compensating *crema al mascarpone.*

[*He sits in the chair and eats greedily.*]

MOZART: I was there when I was a boy: they absolutely adored me. I had more kisses than you've had cakes! . . . When I was a child people loved me.

SALIERI: Perhaps they will again. Why don't you go to London and try?

MOZART: Because I have a wife and child and no money. I wrote to Papa to take the boy off my hands just for a few months so I could go—and he refused! . . . He's a bitter man, of course. After he'd finished showing me off around Europe he never went anywhere himself. He just stayed up in Salzburg year after year, kissing the ring of the fartbishop and lecturing me! . . . [*Confidentally*] The real thing is, you see, he's jealous. Under everything he's jealous of *me*! He'll never forgive me for being cleverer than he is.

[*He leans excitedly over* SALIERI's *chair like a naughty child.*]

I'll tell you a secret. Leopold Mozart is just a jealous, dried-up old turd. . . . And I actually detest him.

[*He giggles guiltily. The* VENTICELLI *appear quickly, and address* SALIERI, *as* MOZART *freezes.*]

V.1: [*Solemnly*]. Leopold Mozart—
V.2: [*Solemnly*]. Leopold Mozart—
V.1 & V.2: Leopold Mozart is dead!

[*They go off.* MOZART *recoils. A long pause.*]

SALIERI: Do not despair. Death is inevitable, my friend.

MOZART: [*Desperately*]. How will I go now?

SALIERI: What do you mean?

MOZART: In the world. There's no one else. No one who understands the wickedness around. *I can't see it!* . . . He watched for me all my life—and I betrayed him.

SALIERI: No!

MOZART: I talked against him.

SALIERI: No!

MOZART: [Distressed]. I married where he begged me not. I left him alone. I danced and played billiards and fooled about, and he sat by himself night after night in an empty house, and no woman to care for him. . . . *Oh, God!*

[SALIERI *rises in concern.*]

SALIERI: Wolfgang. My dear Wolfgang. Don't accuse yourself! . . . Lean upon me, if you care to. . . . Lean upon me!

[SALIERI *opens his arms in a wide gesture of paternal benevolence.* MOZART *approaches him and is almost tempted to surrender to the embrace. But at the last moment he avoids it and brakes away down front, to fall on his knees.*]

MOZART: *Papa!*

SALIERI: So rose the Ghost Father in *Don Giovanni!*

SCENE 9

[*The two grim chords which open the overture to Don Giovanni sound through the
theater.* MOZART *seems to quail under them,
as he stares out front. On the backdrop in
the Light Box appears the silhouette of a
giant black figure, in cloak and tricorne
hat. It extends its arms, menacingly and
engulfingly, toward its begetter.*]

SALIERI: [*To audience*]. A father more accusing
than any in opera. So rose the figure of a
Guilty Libertine cast into Hell. I looked on
astounded as from his ordinary life he made
his art. We were both ordinary men, he and
I. Yet from the ordinary he created Legends—
and I from Legends created only the ordinary!
[*He stands over the kneeling and agonized*
MOZART.] Could I not have stopped my war?
Shown him some pity? ... Oh, yes, my
friends, at any time—if He above had shown
me one drop of it! Every day I sat to work I
prayed—I still prayed, you understand! [*We
hear the exquisite strains of the terzetto*

"*Soave il Vento*" *from* Così *fan tutte.*] [*Calling upward*] "Make this one good in my ears! Just this one! ONE!" [*To audience*] But would He, ever? . . . I heard my music calmed in convention, not one breath of spirit to lift it off the shallows. And I heard *his*—month after month [*The music grows louder*]—the spirit singing through it, unstoppable, to my ears alone! [*To God, in anguish*] Grant this to me! Grant this to me! . . . [*As "God"*] "No, no, no: I do not need you, Salieri. I have Mozart! Better for you to be silent!" *Hahahahahaha!* [*The music cuts off.*] The Creature's dreadful giggle was the laughter of God. . . . I had to end it! But how?

[*He regards the audience with an icy stare.*] There was only one way. *Starvation.* Reduce the man to destitution. Starve out the God!

SCENE 10

Vienna and the Palace of Schönbrunn.

[MOZART *rises, still clutching his stomach.*]

SALIERI: [To MOZART]. How do you fare today?

MOZART: Badly. I have no money, and no prospect of any.

SALIERI: It would not be too hard, surely.

[*Lights up on the Palace of Schönbrunn. The* EMPEROR *stands in the Light Box, in his golden space.*]

JOSEPH: We must find him a post.

SALIERI: [To audience]. One danger! The Emperor. [SALIERI *goes upstage to* JOSEPH.] There's nothing available, Majesty.

JOSEPH: There's Chamber Composer, now that Gluck is dead.

SALIERI: [Shocked]. Mozart to follow Gluck?

JOSEPH: I won't have him say I drove him away. You know what a tongue he has.

SALIERI: Then grant him Gluck's post, Majesty, but not his salary. That would be wrong.

JOSEPH: Gluck got two thousand florins a year. What should Mozart get?

SALIERI: Two hundred. Light payment, yes, but for light duties.

JOSEPH: Perfectly fair. I'm obliged to you, Court Composer.

SALIERI: [Bowing]. Majesty. [To audience] And so easily done. Like many men obsessed with being thought generous, Joseph the Second was quintessentially stingy.

[MOZART kneels to the EMPEROR.]

JOSEPH: Herr Mozart, vous nous faites honneur! [Lights down on JOSEPH, but he stays where he is in the Light Box. MOZART and SALIERI come downstage.]

MOZART: It's a damned insult. Not enough to keep a mouse in cheese for a week!

SALIERI: Regard it as a token, caro Herr.

MOZART: When I was young they gave me snuffboxes. Now it's tokens! And for what? Pom-pom for fireworks! Twang-twang for contredanzes!

SALIERI: I'm sorry it's made you angry. I'd not have suggested it if I'd known you'd be distressed.

MOZART: You suggested it?

SALIERI: I regret I was not able to do more.

MOZART: Oh . . . forgive me! You're a good man! I see that now! You're a truly kind man—and I'm a monstrous fool!

[*He grasps* SALIERI's *hand.*]

SALIERI: No, please . . .

MOZART: You make me ashamed. . . . You excellent man!

SALIERI: No, no, no, no, no—*s'il vous plaît.* A little less enthusiasm, I beg you!

[MOZART *laughs delightedly at this imitation of the* EMPEROR. SALIERI *joins in.* MOZART *suddenly doubles over in pain. He groans shortly.*]

SALIERI: *Wolfgang!* What is it?

MOZART: Nothing. . . . I get cramps sometimes in my stomach. Quite painful. . . .

SALIERI: I'm sorry.

MOZART: Excuse me. . . . It's nothing really.

SALIERI: I will see you soon again?

MOZART: Of course.

SALIERI: Why not visit me?

MOZART: I will. . . . I promise!

SALIERI: *Bene.*

MOZART: *Bene.*

SALIERI: My friend. My new friend!

[MOZART *giggles with pleasure and goes off. A pause.*]

[*To audience*] And I had him. . . . Now, if ever, was the moment for God to crush me. I waited—and do you know what happened? I had just ruined Mozart's career at court. God rewarded me by granting my dearest wish!

[*The* VENTICELLI *come on.*]

V.1: Kapellmeister Bonno.

V.2: Kapellmeister Bonno.

V.1 & V.2: *Kapellmeister Bonno is dead!*

[SALIERI *opens his mouth in surprise.*]

V.1: You are appointed—

V.2: By royal decree—

V.1: To fill his place.

[*Lights full up on the* EMPEROR, *at the back. He is flanked by* STRACK *and* ORSINI-ROSENBERG, *standing like icons, as at their first appearance.*]

JOSEPH: [*Formally, as* SALIERI *turns and bows to him*]. First Royal and Imperial Kapellmeister to our court.

[*The* VENTICELLI *applaud.*]

V.1: Bravo.

V.2: Bravo.

ROSENBERG: *Evviva,* Salieri!

STRACK: Well done, Salieri!

JOSEPH: [*Warmly*]. Dear Salieri. There it is!

[*The lights go down on Schönbrunn. In the dark, the* EMPEROR *and his* COURT *leave the stage for the last time.* SALIERI *turns around, alarmed.*]

SALIERI: [*To audience*]. I was now truly alarmed. How long would I go unpunished?

V.1: Mozart looks appalling.

V.2: It must be galling, of course.

V.1: I hear he's dosing himself constantly with medicine.

SALIERI: For what?

V.2: Envy, I imagine.

SCENE 11

The Prater

[*Fresh green trees appear on the backdrop. The light changes to yellow, turning the blue surround into a rich verdant green. MOZART and CONSTANZE enter arm in arm. She is palpably pregnant and wears a poor coat and bonnet. His clothes are poorer, too, and his manner is hectic. SALIERI promenades with the VENTICELLI.*]

SALIERI: I met him next in the Prater.

MOZART: [*To* SALIERI]. Congratulations, sir!

SALIERI: I thank you. And to you both! [*To audience*] Clearly there was a change for the worse. His eyes gleamed, oddly, like a dog's when the light catches. [*To* MOZART] I hear you are not well, my friend.

[*He acknowledges* CONSTANZE, *who curtsies to him.*]

MOZART: I'm not. My pains stay with me.

SALIERI: How wretched. What can they be?

MOZART: Also, I sleep badly. . . . I have . . . bad dreams.

CONSTANZE: [*Warningly*]. Wolferl!

SALIERI: Dreams?

MOZART: Always the same one: a figure comes to me, wrapped in gray, doing this. [*Beckoning slowly*] It has no face—like a mask! What can it mean, do you think?

SALIERI: Surely you do not believe in dreams?

MOZART: No, of course not—really!

SALIERI: Surely you do not, Madame?

CONSTANZE: I never dream, sir. Things are unpleasant enough to me, awake.

[SALIERI *bows.*]

MOZART: It's all fancy, of course!

CONSTANZE: [*Coldly*]. If Wolfgang had proper work, he might dream less, First Kapellmeister.

MOZART: [*Embarrassed, taking her arm*]. Stanzi, please! . . . Excuse us, sir. . . . Come, dearest. We are well enough, thank you.

[*Husband and wife continue their walk, and halt at the side of the stage. The light grows less sunny.* CONSTANZE *helps* WOLFGANG *off with his coat. He is revealed as wearing a Masonic apron.* CONSTANZE *leaves the stage.*]

V.1: He's growing freakish.

V.2: No question.

V.1: Gray figures with no faces!

SALIERI: [*Looking at him*]. His circumstances make him anxious, I fancy.

V.1: They've moved house again.

V.2: To the Rauhensteingasse. Number 970.

V.1: They must be desperate.

V.2: It's a real slum.

SALIERI: Does he earn any money at all, apart from his post?

V.1: Nothing whatever.

V.2: I hear he's starting to beg.

V.1: They say he's written letters to twenty brother Masons.

SALIERI: Really?

V.2: And they're giving him money.

SALIERI: [*To audience*]. Of course! They *would*! . . . I had *forgotten* the Masons! *Naturally* they would relieve him—how *stupid* of me! . . . There could be no finally starving him with the Masons there to help! As long as he asked they would keep supplying his wants! . . . How could I stop it? And quickly! . . .

V.1: Lord Fugue is most displeased with him!

SALIERI: *Is* he?

SCENE 12

A Masonic Lodge

[A huge golden emblem, descends, encrusted with Masonic symbols.
Enter VAN SWIETEN. He, too, is wearing the
ritual apron over his sober clothes. The
two men clasp hands in fraternal greeting.]

VAN SWIETEN: [Gravely]. This is not good, Brother.
The lodge was not created for you to beg
from.

MOZART: What else can I do?

VAN SWIETEN: Give concerts, as you used to do.

MOZART: I have no subscribers left, Baron. I am
no longer fashionable.

VAN SWIETEN: I am not surprised! You write
tasteless comedies which give offense. I
warned you, often enough.

MOZART: [Humbly]. You did. I admit it.

VAN SWIETEN: I will send you some fugues of
Bach tomorrow. You can arrange those for
my Sunday concert. You shall have a small
fee.

MOZART: Thank you, Baron.

> [VAN SWIETEN *nods and goes out.* SALIERI *steps forward. He, too, wears the Masonic apron.*]

[*Shouting after* VAN SWIETEN] I cannot live by arranging Bach!

SALIERI: [*Sarcastically*]. A generous fellow.

MOZART: All the same, I'll have to do it. If he were to turn the lodge against me, I'd be finished. My brother Masons virtually keep me now.

SALIERI: Wolfgang, it's embarrassing, I know— but you must allow me to relieve you also.

MOZART: No!

SALIERI: If it is the duty of a Mason to help— how much more of a friend.

MOZART: Not another word! I would never take money from you. That friendship is worth all the gold in the world. Please—no more of that!

SALIERI: You overwhelm me.

MOZART: I'll manage: you'll see! Things are looking up already. I've had a marvelous proposal from Schikaneder. He's a new member of this lodge.

SALIERI: Schikaneder? The actor?

MOZART: Yes. He owns a theater in the suburbs.

SALIERI: Well, more of a music hall, surely?

MOZART: Yes . . . He wants me to write him a vaudeville—something for ordinary German

people. Isn't that a wonderful idea? . . . He's
offered me half the receipts when we open.

SALIERI: Nothing in advance?

MOZART: He said he couldn't afford anything. I
know it's not much of an offer. But a popular
piece about brotherly love could celebrate
everything we believe as Mason!

SALIERI: It certainly could! . . . Why don't you
put the Masons *into* it?

MOZART: Into an opera? . . . I couldn't.

[SALIERI *laughs, to indicate that he was
simply making a joke.*]

All the same—what an idea!

SALIERI: [*Earnestly*]. Our rituals are secret,
Wolfgang.

MOZART: I needn't copy them exactly. I could
adapt them a little.

SALIERI: Well . . . It would certainly be in a
great cause.

MOZART: Brotherly love!

SALIERI: Brotherly love!

[*They both turn and look solemnly at the
great golden emblem hanging at the back.*]

SALIERI: [*Warmly*]. Take courage, Wolfgang. It's
a glorious idea.

MOZART: It is, isn't it? It really *is*!

SALIERI: Of course say nothing till it's done.

MOZART: Not a word.

SALIERI: [*Making a sign: closed fist*]. Secret!

MOZART: [*Making a similar sign*]. Secret!

SALIERI: Good.

[*He steps out of the scene downstage.*]

[*To audience*]. And if that didn't finish him off with the Masons—nothing would!

[*The gold emblem withdraws. We hear the mercy dance of Monostatos and the hypnotized slaves from The Magic Flute: "Das Klinget, so heimlich, Das Klinget so schön!" To the tinkling of the glockenspiel* SERVANTS *bring in a long plain table loaded with manuscripts and bottles. It also bears a plain upturned stool. They place this in the wooden area head-on to the audience. At the same time* CONSTANZE *appears wearily from the back, and enters this apartment: the Rauhensteingasse.*

Simultaneously upstage left, two other SERVANTS *have placed the little gilded table bearing a loaded cake-stand and three of the gilded chairs from Salieri's resplendent salon. We now have in view the two contrasting apartments.*

As soon as the emblem withdraws, the VENTICELLI *appear to* SALIERI.]

SCENE 13

Mozart's Apartment; Salieri's Apartment

V.1: Mozart is delighted with himself!

V.2: He's writing a secret opera!

V.1: [*Crossly*]. And won't tell anyone its theme.

V.2: It's really too tiresome.

    [*The* VENTICELLI *go off.*]

SALIERI: He told me. He told me everything! . . .
    Initiation ceremonies. Ceremonies with blind-
    folds. All rituals copied from the Masons! . . .
    He sat at home preparing his own destruction.
    A home where life grew daily more grim.

    [*He goes upstage and sits on one of his
    gilded chairs, devouring a cake.* MOZART
    *also sits at his table, wrapped in a blanket,
    and starts to write music. Opposite him*
    CONSTANZE *sits on a stool, wrapped in a
    shawl.*]

CONSTANZE: I'm cold . . . I'm cold all day. . . .
    Hardly surprising since we have no firewood.

MOZART: Papa was right. We end exactly as he
    said. Beggars.

CONSTANZE: It's all his fault.

MOZART: Papa's?

CONSTANZE: He kept you a baby all your life.

MOZART: I don't understand. . . . You always loved Papa.

CONSTANZE: *I* did?

MOZART: You adored him. You told me so often. [*Slight pause*]

CONSTANZE: [*Flatly*]. I hated him.

MOZART: What?

CONSTANZE: And he hated *me*.

MOZART: That's absurd. He loved us both very much. You're being extremely silly now.

CONSTANZE: Am I?

MOZART: [*Airily*]. Yes you are: little-wife-of-my-heart!

CONSTANZE: Do you want to know what I really thought of your father? . . . Do you remember the fire we had last night, because it was so cold you couldn't even get the ink wet? You said "What a blaze," remember? "What a blaze!" All those old papers going up? Well, my dear, those old papers were just all your father's letters, that's all—every one he wrote since the day we married.

MOZART: What?

CONSTANZE: Every one! All the letters about what a ninny I am—what a bad housekeeper I am! Every one!

MOZART: Stanzi!

CONSTANZE: Shit on him! . . . *Shit on him!*

MOZART: *You bitch!*

CONSTANZE: [*Savagely*]. At least it kept us warm! What else will do that? Perhaps we should dance! You love to dance, Wolferl—let's dance! Dance to keep warm! [*Grandly*] Write me a contredanze, Mozart! It's your job to write dances, isn't it?

> [*Hysterical, she snatches up his manuscripts from the table and scatters them over the floor—pulling up her skirts and dancing roughly round the room like a demented peasant, to the tune of "Non più andrai"!*]

CONSTANZE: [*Singing savagely*]. *Non più andrai, farfallone amoroso—notte e giorno d'intorno girando!*

MOZART: [*Shrieking*]. Stop it! Stop it!

[*He rises and tries to sieze her.*] Stanzi-marini! Marini-bini! Don't *please!* . . . Please—please I beg you! . . . Look. There's a kiss! Where's it coming from? Right out of that corner! There's another one—all wet, all sloppy wet, coming straight to you! Kiss—kiss—kiss—kiss!

[*She pushes him roughly away.*]

CONSTANZE: Get off!

[*A long pause*]

MOZART: I'm frightened, Stanzi. . . . Something awful's happening to me.

CONSTANZE: [*Quietly*]. I can't bear it. I can't bear much more of this.

MOZART: [*Absorbed in himself*]. The Figure's like this now—[*Beckoning more urgently*] —Here. Come here. Here ... Its face still hidden. Always hidden.

CONSTANZE: [*Crying out*]. Stop it, for God's sake! Stop it! ... Stop! ... It's me who's frightened. ... Me! ... You frighten me. ... If you go on like this I'll leave you. I swear it.

MOZART: [*Shocked*]. Stanzi!

CONSTANZE: I mean it ... I do. ...

[*She puts her hand to her stomach, as if in pain.*]

MOZART: I'm sorry. ... Oh God, I'm sorry ... I'm sorry, I'm sorry, I'm sorry, I'm sorry! ... Come here to me, little-wife-of-my-heart! Come ... Come ...

[*He kneels and coaxes her to him. She comes half-reluctantly, half-willingly.*]

Who am I? ... Quick: tell me. Hold me and tell who I am. Who?—come on.

CONSTANZE: Pussy-wussy.

MOZART: Who else?

CONSTANZE: Miaowy-powy.

MOZART: And you're squeaky-peeky. And Stanzi-manzi. And Bini-gini!

[*She surrenders.*]

CONSTANZE: Wolfi-polfi!

MOZART: Poopy-peepee!

[*They giggle.*]

CONSTANZE: Now don't be stupid.

MOZART: [Insistent: like a child]. Come on—do it. Do it. . . . Let's do it. "Poppy."

[They play a private game, gradually doing it faster, on their knees.]

CONSTANZE: Poppy.

MOZART: [Changing it]. Pappy.

CONSTANZE: [Copying]. Pappy.

MOZART: Pappa.

CONSTANZE: Pappa.

MOZART: Pappa-pappa!

CONSTANZE: Pappa-pappa!

MOZART: Pappa-pappa-pappa-pappa!

CONSTANZE: Pappa-pappa-pappa-pappa!

[They rub noses.]

TOGETHER: Pappa-pappa-pappa-pappa! Pappa-pappa-pappa-pappa!

CONSTANZE: Ah!

[She suddenly cries out in distress, and clutches her stomach.]

MOZART: Stanzi! . . . Stanzi, what is it?

[The VENTICELLI hurry in.]

SALIERI: And suddenly she was delivered! A boy!

V.2: Poor little imp.

V.1: To be born to that couple.

V.2: In that room.

V.1: With that money.

V.2: And the Father a baby himself.

[During the above, CONSTANZE has slowly risen, and divested herself of her stuffed *apron—thereby ceasing to be pregnant. Now she turns sorrowfully and walks slowly upstage and off it.* MOZART *follows her for a few steps, alarmed. He halts.*]

V.1: And now I hear—

V.2: Now I hear—

V.1: Something more has happened.

V.2: Even stranger.

[MOZART *picks up a bottle, then moves swiftly into Salieri's room.*]

MOZART: She's gone!

SALIERI: What do you mean?

[*The* VENTICELLI *slip away.*]

MOZART: Constanze's gone away. Just for a while, she says. She's taken the baby and gone to Baden. To the spa. It'll cost us the last money we had.

SALIERI: But *why?*

MOZART: She's right to go. It's my fault. She thinks I'm mad.

SALIERI: Surely not?

MOZART: Perhaps I am. I think I am. Last night I saw the Figure again—the Figure in my dreams.

SALIERI: Wolfgang—

MOZART: It stood before my table, its face still gray, still masked. But this time it spoke to me. "Wolfgang Mozart—you must write now a Requiem Mass. Take up your pen and begin!"

SALIERI: A Requiem?

MOZART: I asked "Who has died? Who is this Requiem for?" It turned and left the room.

SALIERI: Oh, this is morbid fancy, my friend!

MOZART: It had the force of real things! . . . To tell the truth—I do not know whether it happened in my head or out of it. . . . No wonder Stanzi has gone. I frightened her away. . . . And now she'll miss the vaudeville.

SALIERI: You mean it's finished? So soon?

MOZART: Oh yes—music is easy: it's marriage that's hard!

SALIERI: I long to see it.

MOZART: Would you come, truly? The theater isn't grand. No one from court will be there.

SALIERI: Do you think that matters to me? I would travel anywhere for a work by you! . . . I am no subtitute for your little wife—but I know someone who could be!

[He gets up. MOZART rises also.]

MOZART: Who?

SALIERI: I'll tell you what—I'll bring Katherina! She'll cheer you up!

MOZART: Katherina!

SALIERI: As I remember it, you quite enjoyed her company!

[MOZART laughs heartily. CAVALIERI enters, now fatter and wearing an elaborate plumed hat. She curtsies to MOZART and takes his arm.]

MOZART: [Bowing]. Signora!

SALIERI: [To audience]. And so to the opera we went—a strange band of three!

[The other two freeze.]

The First Kapellmeister—sleek as a cat. His mistress—now fat and feathered like the great song-bird she'd become. And demented Mozart—drunk on the cheap wine which was now his constant habit.

[They unfreeze.]

We went out into the suburbs—to a crowded music hall—in a slum!

SCENE 14

The Theater by the Weiden

[Two benches are brought in and placed down front. Sudden noise. A crowd of working-class Germans swarms in from the back: a chattering mass of humanity through which the three have to push their way to the front. The long table is pushed horizontally, and the rowdy audience piles on top

*of it, smoking pipes and chewing sausages.
Unobserved, BARON VAN SWIETEN comes in
also, and stands at the back.]*

MOZART: You must be indulgent now! It's my
first piece of this kind!

*[The three sit on the first bench: MOZART
sick and emaciated; CAVALIERI blousy and
bedizened; SALIERI as elegant as ever.]*

SALIERI: We sat as he wished us to, among ordinary Germans! The smell of sweat and sau-
sage was almost annihilating!

*[CAVALIERI presses a mouchoir to her sensi-
tive nose.]*

[To Mozart] This is so exciting!

MOZART: *[Happily]*. Do you think so?

SALIERI: *[Looking about him]*. Oh yes! This is
exactly the audience we should be writing
for! Not the dreary court . . . As always—you
show the way!

[The audience freezes.]

[To us] As always, he did. My pungent neigh-
bors rolled on their benches at the jokes—

*[They unfreeze, briefly, to demonstrate this
mirth.]*

And I alone, in their midst, heard—The Magic
Flute.

*[They freeze again. The great hymn at the
end of Act 2 is heard: "Heil sei euch
Geweihten."]*

He had put the Masons into it right enough.

Oh yes—but how? He had turned them into an order of Eternal Priests. I heard voices calling out of ancient temples. I saw a vast sun rise on a timeless land, where animals danced and children floated, and by its rays all the poisons we feed each other drawn up and burnt away!

[*A great sun does indeed rise inside the Light Box, and standing in it the gigantic silhouette of a priestly figure extending its arms to the world in universal greeting.*]

And in this sun—behold—I saw his *father*! No more an accusing figure but forgiving!— the highest priest of the Order—his hand extended to the world in love! Wolfgang feared Leopold no longer: a final legend had been made! . . . Oh, the sound—the sound of that new-found peace in him—mocking my undiminishing pain! There was the Magic Flute— there beside me!

[*He points to* MOZART. *Applause from all.* MOZART *jumps up excitedly onto the bench and acknowledges it with arms flung out. He turns, a bottle in his hand, his eyes staring, and all freeze again.*]

Mozart the flute and God the relentless player! How long could the Creature stand it—so frail, so palpably mortal? And what was this I was tasting suddenly? Could it be pity? . . . Never!

VAN SWIETEN: [*Calling out*]. Mozart!

    [VAN SWIETEN *pushes his way to the front through the crowd of dispersing* CITIZENS. *He is outraged.*]

MOZART: [*Turning joyfully to greet him*]. Baron! You here! How wonderful of you to come!

SALIERI: [*To audience*]. I had of course suggested it.

VAN SWIETEN: [*With cold fury*]. What have you done?

MOZART: Excellency?

VAN SWIETEN: You have put our rituals into a vulgar show!

MOZART: No, sir—

VAN SWIETEN: They are plain for all to see! And to laugh at! You have betrayed the Order.

MOZART: [*In horror*]. No!

SALIERI: Baron, a word with you—

VAN SWIETEN: Don't speak for him, Salieri! [*To* MOZART, *with frozen contempt*] You were ever a cruel vulgarian we hoped to mend. Stupid, hopeless task! Now you are a betrayer as well. I shall never forgive you. And depend upon it—I shall ensure that no Freemason or person of distinction will do so in Vienna so long as I have life!

SALIERI: Baron, please, I must speak!

VAN SWIETEN: No, sir! Leave, alone. [*To* MOZART] I did not look for this reward, Mozart. Never speak to me.

[He goes out. CAVALIERI, embarrassed, goes out another way. The lights change. The benches are taken off. SALIERI watches MOZART, who stands as one dead.]

SCENE 15

SALIERI: Wolfgang? . . .
[MOZART shakes his head sharply—and walks away from him, upstage, desolate and stunned.]
Wolfgang—all is not lost.
[MOZART enters his apartment, and freezes.]
[To audience] But of course it was! Now he was ruined. Broken and shunned by all men of influence. He did not even get his half receipts from the opera.
[The VENTICELLI come in.]
V.1: Schikaneder pays him nothing.
V.2: Schikaneder cheats him.
V.1: Gives him enough for liquor.
V.2: And keeps all the rest.
SALIERI: I couldn't have managed it better myself.
[MOZART takes up a blanket and muffles himself in it. Then he sits at his work-

table, down front, staring out at the audience, quite still, the blanket almost over his face.] And then silence. No word came from him at all. Why? ... I waited each day. Nothing. Why? ... [To the VENTICELLI, brusquely] What does he do?

[MOZART writes.]

V.1: He sits at his window.

V.2: All day and all night.

V.1: Writing—

V.2: Writing—like a man possessed.

[MOZART springs to his feet, and freezes.]

V.1: Springs up every moment!

V.2: Stares wildly at the street!

V.1: Expecting something—

V.2: Someone—

V.1 & V.2: We can't imagine what!

SALIERI: [To audience]. I could!

[He also springs up excitedly, dismissing the VENTICELLI. MOZART and SALIERI now both stand staring out front.]

Who did he look for? A Figure in gray, masked and sorrowing, come to take him away. I knew what he was doing, alone in that slum! He was writing his Requiem Mass—for himself! ... And now I confess the wickedest thing I did to him.

[His VALET brings him the clothes which he describes, and he puts them on, turning

*his back to us to don the hat—to which is
attached a mask.*]

My friends—there is no blasphemy a man
will not commit, compelled to such a war as
mine! I got me a cloak of gray. Yes. And a
mask of gray—Yes!

[*He turns around: he is masked.*]

And appeared myself to the demented Creature as—the Messenger of God! . . . I confess
that in November, 1791, I—Antonio Salieri,
then as now First Kapellmeister to the Empire—
walked empty Vienna in the freezing moon-
light for seven nights on end! That precisely
as the clocks of the city struck one I would
halt beneath Mozart's window—and become
his more terrible clock.

[*The clock strikes one.* SALIERI, *without
moving from the left side of the stage, raises
his arms: his fingers show seven days.*
MOZART *rises—fascinated and appalled—
and stands equally rigid on the right side,
looking out.*]

Every night I showed him one day less—then
stalked away. Every night the face he showed
me at the glass was more crazed at each
visitation. Finally— with no days left to him—
horror! I arrived as usual. Halted. And instead of fingers, reached up beseechingly as
the Figure of his dreams! [*Urging*] "Come!—
Come!—Come! . . ."

[*He beckons to* MOZART, *insidiously.*]

He stood swaying, as if he would faint off into death. But suddenly—incredibly—he realized all his little strength, and in a clear voice called down to me the words out of his opera *Don Giovanni*, inviting the statue to dinner.

MOZART: [*Pushing open the "window"*]. *O statua gentilissima, venite a cena!*

[*He beckons in his turn.*]

SALIERI: For a long moment one terrified man looked at another. Then—unbelievably—I found myself nodding, just as in the opera. Starting to move across the street!

[*The rising and falling scale passage from the Overture to Don Giovanni sounds darkly, looped in sinister repetition. To this hollow music* SALIERI *marches slowly upstage.*]

Pushing down the latch of his door—tramping up the stairs with stone feet. There was no stopping it. *I was in his dream!*

[MOZART *stands terrified by his table.* SALIERI *throws open the door. An instant light change.*]

SCENE 16

Mozart's Apartment

[SALIERI *stands still, staring impassively downstage.* MOZART *addresses him in awe.*]

MOZART: It's not finished! ... Not nearly! ... Forgive me. Time was I could write a Mass in a week! ... Give me one month more, and it'll be done: I swear it! ... He'll grant me that, surely? God can't want it unfinished! ... Look—look, see what I've done.

[*He snatches up the pages from the table and brings them eagerly to the* FIGURE.]

Here's the Kyrie—that's finished! Take that to Him—He'll see it's not unworthy! ...

[*Unwillingly* SALIERI *moves across the room, takes the pages, and sits behind the table in* MOZART's *chair, staring out front.*]

Grant me time, I beg you! If you do, I swear I'll write a real piece of music. I know I've boasted I've written hundreds, but it's not true. I've written nothing finally good!

[SALIERI *looks at the pages. Immediately we hear the somber opening of the Requiem Mass. Over this* MOZART *speaks.*]

Oh, it began so well, my life. Once the world was so full, so happy! . . . All the journeys—all the carriages—all the rooms of smiles! Everyone smiled at me once—the king at Schönbrunn; the princess at Versailles—they lit my way with candles to the clavier—my father bowing, bowing, bowing with such joy! . . . "Chevalier Mozart, my miraculous son!" . . . Why has it all gone? . . . Why? . . . Was I so bad? So wicked? . . . Answer for Him and tell me!

[*Deliberately* SALIERI *tears the paper into halves. The music stops instantly. Silence.*]

[*Fearfully*] Why? . . . Is it not good?

SALIERI: [*Stiffly*]. It is good. Yes. It is good.

[*He tears off a corner of the music paper, elevates it in the manner of the Communion Service, places it on his tongue and eats it.*]

[*In pain*] I eat what God gives me. Dose after dose. For all of life. His poison. We are both poisoned, Amadeus. I with you: you with me.

[*In horror,* MOZART *moves slowly behind him, placing his hand over* SALIERI's *mouth—then, still from behind, slowly removes the mask and hat.* SALIERI *stares at us.*]

Ecco mi. Antonio Salieri. Ten years of my hate have poisoned you to death.

[MOZART *falls to his knees, by the table.*]

MOZART: Oh God!

SALIERI: [Contemptuously]. God?! . . . God will not help you! God does not help!

MOZART: Oh God! . . . Oh God! . . . Oh God!

SALIERI: God does not love you, Amadeus! God does not love! He can only use! . . . He cares nothing for whom He uses: nothing for whom He denies! . . . You are no use to Him anymore. You're too weak—too sick! He has finished with you! All you can do now is die!

MOZART: *Ah!*

[*With a groan* MOZART *crawls quickly through the trestle of the table, like an animal finding a burrow—or a child a safe place of concealment.* SALIERI *kneels by the table, calling in at his victim in desperation.*]

SALIERI: Die, Amadeus! Die, I beg you, die! . . . Leave me alone, *ti imploro!* Leave me alone at last! Leave me alone!

[*He beats on the table in his despair.*]

Alone! Alone! Alone! Alone!

MOZART: [Crying out at the top of his lungs]. PAPAAAAA!

[*He freezes—his mouth open in the act of screaming—his head staring out from under the table, a gargoyle of fear.* SALIERI *rises in horror. Silence. Very slowly,* MOZART

140

crawls out from under the table. He stares
upward. He sits. He smiles.]

[In a childish voice] Papa!

[Silence]

Papa . . . Papa . . .

[He extends his arms; imploringly. He
speaks as a very young boy.]

Take me, Papa. Take me. Put down your
arms and I'll hop into them. Just as we used
to do it! . . . Hop-hop-hop-hop-UP!

[He jumps up onto the table. SALIERI watches
in horror.]

Hold me close to you, Papa. Let's sing our little
kissing song together. Do you remember? . . .

[He sings in an infantine voice.]

Oragna figata fa! Marina gamina fa!

SALIERI: [Quietly]. Reduce the man: reduce
the God. Behold my vow fulfilled. The pro-
foundest voice in the world reduced to a
nursery tune.

[He leaves the room, slowly, as MOZART
resumes his singing.]

MOZART: *Oragna figata fa! Marina gamina fa!*

[As SALIERI withdraws, CONSTANZE appears
from the back of the stage, her bonnet in
her hand. She has returned from Baden.
She comes downstage toward her husband,
and finds him there on the table singing in
an obviously childish treble.]

Oragna figata fa! Marina gamina fa. Fa! Fa!

[*He kisses the air, several times. Finally he becomes aware of his wife standing beside him.*]

MOZART: [*Uncertainly*]. Stanzi?

CONSTANZE: Wolfi? . . .

MOZART: [*In relief*]. Stanzi!

CONSTANZE: [*With great tenderness*]. Wolfi—my love! Little husband of my heart!

[*He virtually falls off the table into her arms.*]

MOZART: *Oh!*

[*He clings to her in overwhelming pleasure. She helps him gently to move around the table to the chair behind it, facing out front.*]

CONSTANZE: Oh, my dear one—come with me. Come on . . . Come on now. There . . . There . . .

[*MOZART sits weakly.*]

MOZART: [*Like a child still, and most earnestly.*] Salieri . . . Salieri has killed me.

CONSTANZE: Yes, my dear.

[*Practically, she busies herself clearing the table of its candle, its bottle and its inkwell.*]

MOZART: He has! . . . He told me so! . . .

CONSTANZE: Yes, yes: I'm sure.

[*She finds two pillows and places them at the left-hand head of the table.*]

MOZART: [*Petulantly*]. He did. He did! . . .

CONSTANZE: Hush now, lovey.

[*She helps her dying husband onto the*

142

table, now his bed. He lies down, and she covers him with her shawl.]

I'm back to take care of you. I'm sorry I went away. I'm here now, for always!

MOZART: Salieri . . . Salieri . . . Salieri . . . Salieri!

[*He starts to weep.*]

CONSTANZE: Oh lovey, be silent now. No one has hurt you. You'll get better soon, I promise. Can you hear me?

[*Faintly the Lacrimosa of the Requiem Mass beings to sound.* MOZART *rises to hear it— leaning against his wife's shoulder. His hand begins feebly to beat out drum measures from the music. During the whole of the following it is evident that he is composing the Mass in his head, and does not hear his wife at all.*]

You've got to get well, Wolfi—because we need you. Karl and baby Franz as well. There's only three of us, lovey: we don't cost much. Just don't leave us—we wouldn't know what to do without you. And you wouldn't know much either, up in Heaven, without us. You soppy thing. You can't even cut up your own meat without help! . . . I'm not clever, lovey. It can't have been easy living with a goose. But I've looked after you, you must admit that. And I've given you fun too—quite a lot really! . . . Are you listening?

[*The drum strokes get slower, and stop.*]

Know one thing. It was the best day of my life when you married me. And as long as I live I'll be the most honored woman in the world. . . . Can you hear me?

[She becomes aware that MOZART is dead. She opens her mouth in a silent scream, raising her arm in a rigid gesture of grief. The great chord of the "Amen" does not resolve itself, but lingers on in intense reverberation.

CITIZENS of Vienna come in, dressed in black, from the right. CONSTANZE kneels and freezes in grief, as SERVANTS come in and stand at each of the four corners of the table on which the dead body lies. VAN SWIETEN also comes in.]

SALIERI: [Hard]. The Death Certificate said kidney failure, hastened by exposure to cold. Generous Lord Fugue paid for a pauper's funeral. Twenty other corpses. An unmarked limepit.

[VAN SWIETEN approaches CONSTANZE.]

VAN SWIETEN: What little I can spare, you shall have for the children. There's no need to waste it on vain show.

[The SERVANTS lift the table and bear it, with its burden, upstage center, to the Light Box. The CITIZENS follow it.]

SALIERI: What did I feel? Relief, of course: I confess it. And pity too, for the man I helped to destroy. I felt the pity God can never feel. I weakened God's flute to thinness. God blew— as He must—without cease. The flute split in the mouth of His insatiable need.

[*The* CITIZENS *kneel. In dead silence the* SERVANTS *throw* MOZART's *body off the table into space at the back of the stage.*

All depart save SALIERI *and* CONSTANZE. *She unfreezes and starts assiduously collecting the manuscripts scattered over the floor.*

SALIERI *now speaks with an increasingly aging voice: a voice poisoned more and more by his own bitterness.*]

As for Constanze, in the fullness of time she married again—a Danish diplomat as dull as a clock—and retired to Salzburg, birthplace of the Composer, to become the pious Keeper of his Shrine!

[CONSTANZE *rises, wrapping her shawl about her, and clasping manuscripts to her bosom.*]

CONSTANZE: [*Reverentially*]. A sweeter-tongued man never lived! In ten years of blissful marriage I never heard him utter a single coarse or conceited word. The purity of his life is reflected absolutely in the purity of his music! . . . [*More briskly*] In selling his manuscripts I charge by the ink. So many notes, so many schillings. That seems to me the simplest way.

[*She leaves the stage, a pillar of rectitude.*]

SCENE 17

SALIERI: One amazing fact emerged. Mozart did not *imagine* that masked Figure who said "Take up your pen and write a Requiem." It was *real!* . . . A certain bizarre nobleman called Count Walsegg had a longing to be thought a composer. He actually sent his steward in disguise to Mozart to commission the piece—secretly, so that he could pass it off as his own work. And this he even did! After Mozart's death it was actually performed as Count Walsegg's Requiem. . . . And I conducted it.

[*He smiles at the audience.*]

Naturally I did. In those days I presided over all great musical occasions.

[*He divests himself of his cloak.*]

I even conducted the salvos of cannon in Beethoven's dreadful *Battle Symphony*. The experience left me almost as deaf as *he* was!

[*The* CITIZENS *bow and kiss their hands to him.*]

I remained in Vienna—City of Musicians—

reverenced by all. And slowly I understood the nature of God's punishment! ... What had I begged for in that church as a boy? Was it not *fame*? ... Fame for excellence? ... Well now I had fame! I was to become—quite simply—the most famous musician in Europe!
[*All the* CITIZENS *fall on their knees before him, clapping their hands silently, and relentlessly extending their arms upward and upward almost obliterating him.*]
I was to be bricked up in fame! Embalmed in fame! Buried in fame—but for work I knew to be *absolutely worthless!* This was my sentence: I must endure thirty years of being called "Distinguished" by people incapable of distinguishing! ... And finally—His master-stroke! When my nose had been rubbed in fame to vomiting—it would all be taken away from me. Every scrap.
[*The* CITIZENS *rise, and all walk away indifferently upstage, past him, and on into the Light Box, and off the stage.*]
I must survive to see myself become extinct!
[*A* SERVANT *hands him his old stained dressing gown and cap.*]
When they trundled me out in a carriage to get my last award, a man on the curb said, "Isn't that one of the generals from Waterloo?"
[*The last movement of the "Jupiter" Symphony begins to sound, growing ever louder.*]

Mozart's music sounded louder and louder through the world! And mine faded completely, till no one played it at all!

[*The Mozart symphony wells to a huge crescendo, seeming to drown* SALIERI. *He sinks to his knees under the weight of it, and finally claps his hands to his aching ears to shut it out. The deafening music snaps off. The curtain descends in a rush. A clock strikes six.*]

SCENE 18

Salieri's Apartment: November 1823

[*A* SERVANT *comes in quickly with the wheelchair.* SALIERI *speaks again in the voice of an old man.*]

SALIERI: [*To audience*]. Dawn has come. I must release you—and myself. One moment's violence and it's done. You see, I cannot accept this. I did not live on earth to be His joke for eternity. I *will* be remembered! *I will be remembered!*—if not in fame, than infamy.

One moment more and I win my battle with Him. Watch and see! . . . All this month I've been shouting about murder. "Have mercy, Mozart! Pardon your Assassin!" . . . And now my last move. A false confession—short and convincing!

[*He pulls it out of his pocket.*]

How I really did murder Mozart—with arsenic—out of envy! And how I cannot live another day under the knowledge! By tonight they'll hear out there how I died—and they'll believe it's true! . . . Let them forget me then. For the rest of time whenever men say Mozart with love, they will say Salieri with loathing! . . . *I am getting to be immortal after all!* And He is powerless to prevent it.

[*To God*] So, Signore—see now if man is mocked!

[*The VALET comes in with a tray, bearing a bowl of hot shaving water, soap and a razor. He sets this on the table. SALIERI hands him the confession.*]

[*To VALET*] Good morning. Lay this on the desk in the cabinet. Append your name to it in witness that this is my hand. *Via—subito!*

[*The man takes the paper and goes, bewildered, upstage right. SALIERI picks up the razor, and rises. He addresses the audience most simply and directly.*]

SALIERI: *Amici cari.* I was born a pair of ears

and nothing else. It is only through hearing music that I know God exists. Only through writing music that I could worship ... All around me men seek liberty for mankind. I sought only slavery for myself. To be owned—ordered—exhausted by an *Absolute*. Music. This was denied me, and with it all meaning.

[*He opens the razor.*]

Now I go to become a ghost myself. I will stand in the shadows when you come here to this earth in your turns. And when you feel the dreadful bite of your failures—and hear the taunting of unachievable, uncaring God—I will whisper my name to you: "Salieri: Patron Saint of Mediocrities!" And in the depth of your downcastness you can pray to me. And I will forgive you. *Vi saluto.*

[*He cuts his throat, and falls backwards into the wheelchair. The* COOK—*who has just come in, carrying a plate of fresh buns for breakfast, sees this and screams. The* VALET *rushes in at the same time from the other side. Together they pull the wheelchair, with its slumped body, backward upstage, and anchor it in the center. The* VENTICELLI *appear again, in the costume of 1823.*]

SCENE 19

V.1: Beethoven's Conversation Book, November 1823. Visitors write the news for the deaf man.

[*He hands a book to* VENTICELLO TWO.]

V.2: [*Reading*]. "Salieri has cut his throat—but is still alive!"

[SALIERI *stirs and comes to life, looking about him bewilderedly. The* VALET *and the* COOK *depart. He stares out front at us astounded.*]

V.1: Beethoven's Conversation Book, 1824. Visitors write the news for the deaf man.

[*He hands another book to* VENTICELLO TWO.]

V.2: [*Reading*]. "Salieri is quite deranged. He keeps claiming that he is guilty of Mozart's death, and made away with him by poison."

[*The light narrows into a bright cone, beating on* SALIERI.]

V.1: The German Musical Times, May 25th, 1825.

[*He hands a newspaper to* VENTICELLO TWO.]

V.2: [*Reading*]. "Our worthy Salieri just cannot die. In the frenzy of his imagination he is even said to accuse himself of complicity in Mozart's early death. A rambling of the mind believed in truth by no one but the deluded old man himself.''

[*The music stops.* SALIERI *stares ahead in pain.*]

V.1: I don't believe it.

V.2: I don't believe it.

V.1: I don't believe it.

V.2: I don't believe it.

V.1 & V.2: *No one believes it in the world!*

[*They go off. The light dims a little.* SALIERI *stirs—rises, and looks out far into the darkness of the theater.*]

SALIERI: Mediocrities everywhere—now and to come—I absolve you all. Amen!

[*He extends his arms upward and outward to embrace the assembled audience in a wide gesture of benediction—finally folding his arms high across his own breast in a gesture of self-sanctification.*

The light fades completely. The last four chords of the Masonic Funeral Music of AMADEUS MOZART *sound throughout the theater.*]

END OF PLAY

SALIERI'S MARCH as played by both Salieri and Mozart,
Mozart playing it faster, lighter, and less decoratively.

MOZART'S TRANSFORMATION
PROCESS:

"That fourth doesn't
quite work, does it?"

"Let's try the third
above . . . . . ."

"Ah! . . ."

"NON PIU ANDRAI" arranged for piano by Kevin Leeman

At first tentatively

About the Author

Peter Shaffer was born in Liverpool, England, in 1926. During the Second World War he worked as a conscript in a coal mine; later he studied history on a scholarship to Cambridge University, and departed thence to New York. There he worked in a Doubleday bookstore, and the Forty-second Street library, living for much of the time in Hell's Kitchen, and returning three years later to London convinced of his own unemployability. In some desperation he wrote his first play, *Five Finger Exercise*, which was produced in 1958 to widespread approval (in New York in 1959, where it won the Drama Critics Award), thereby relieving him of the necessity of working in other stores or offices.

The success of his first play suggested to Shaffer that he might be a dramatist at heart. Partly because he had no aptitude for doing anything else, he sat down during the ensuing years and produced other plays. All of these met with great success, first in London and then in New York: *The Private Ear* and *The Public Eye*, a double bill, in 1962; *The Royal Hunt of the Sun*, an epic concerning the conquest of Peru, which Bernard Levin described as "the greatest play of our generation," in 1964; and in the following year *Black Comedy*, a romp designed for Britain's National Theatre, which another critic hailed as "the farce of the century." In 1973 Peter Shaffer wrote *Equus*, which ran for over a thousand performances on Broadway, winning the Tony Award and the Drama Critics Award. *Amadeus* is the fourth successful play Shaffer originated at the National Theatre of Great Britain where it is still running. In England it won both the Evening Standard Drama Award and the Theatre Critics Award. *Amadeus* opened on Broadway in December 1980, where its appearance was hailed by Clive Barnes as a total triumph.

Peter Shaffer lives in New York, a city for which he feels a strong and undiminishable passion.

Ⓢ   Ⓢ

Contemporary Plays in SIGNET and
SIGNET CLASSIC Editions

(0451)

☐ **A STREETCAR NAMED DESIRE by Tennessee Williams.** The Pulitzer Prize-winning play of a woman betrayed by love. Illustrated with scenes from the New York, London, and Paris productions. (121805—$2.50)

☐ **CAT ON A HOT TIN ROOF by Tennessee Williams.** A drama of seething passions that beset a Southern family in a shattering moment of revelation. (125878—$2.50)

☐ **FOUR PLAYS BY TENNESSEE WILLIAMS: SUMMER AND SMOKE, ORPHEUS DESCENDING, SUDDENLY LAST SUMMER AND PERIOD OF ADJUSTMENT.** Love, hate, comedy, tragedy, joy, sorrow, passion, violence—all come alive in these four magnificent plays. (518578—$3.95)*

☐ **THREE BY TENNESSEE WILLIAMS: SWEET BIRD OF YOUTH, THE ROSE TATTOO and THE NIGHT OF THE IGUANA,** three of the Pulitzer Prize-winning author's most brilliant plays. (518365—3.95)*

☐ **A RAISIN IN THE SUN by Lorraine Hansberry.** Winner of the 1955–59 New York Drama Critics' Award, it tells the compelling story of a young black father's struggle to break free from the barriers of prejudice. (124154—$1.95)

☐ **TO BE YOUNG, GIFTED AND BLACK: Lorraine Hansberry in Her Own Words.** Adapted by Robert Nemiroff. Introduction by James Baldwin. A unique play woven from selections of Hansberry's published and unpublished works—a major statement on the black experience in America. (110803—$2.50)

*Price is $4.50 in Canada

Buy them at your local

bookstore or use coupon

on next page for ordering.

World Drama from SIGNET CLASSIC

☐ **TARTUFFE and OTHER PLAYS by Molière.** Translated, with an Introduction by Donald M. Fame. Includes *The Ridiculous Précieuses, The School for Husbands, The School for Wives, Don Juan, The Versailles Impromptu,* and *The Critique of The School for Wives.* (515668—$2.95)

☐ **THE MISANTHROPE and OTHER PLAYS by Molière.** Translated, with an Introduction by Donald M. Fame. Includes *The Doctor in Spite of Himself, The Miser, The Would-Be Gentleman, The Mischievious Machinations of Scapin, The Learned Women,* and *The Imaginary Invalid.* (517210—$3.50)

☐ **CHEKHOV: THE MAJOR PLAYS by Anton Chekhov.** *Ivanov, The Sea Gull, Uncle Vanya, The Three Sisters* and *The Cherry Orchard.* New translation by Ann Dunnigan. Foreword by Robert Brustein. (517679—$2.95)

☐ **IBSEN: FOUR MAJOR PLAYS, Volume I, by Henrik Ibsen.** *The Master Builder, A Doll's House, Hedda Gabler,* and *The Wild Duck.* New translation with Foreword by Rolf Fjelde.(513975—$2.25)

☐ **IBSEN: FOUR MAJOR PLAYS, Volume II, by Henrik Ibsen.** *Ghosts, An Enemy of the People, The Lady from the Sea,* and *John Gabriel Borkman.* New translation by Rolf Fjelde. (516559—$2.50)

☐ **PLAYS by George Bernard Shaw,** Introduction by Eric Bentley. *Man and Superman, Candida, Arms and the Man,* and *Mrs. Warren's Profession.* (517865—$3.95)

☐ **PYGMALION and MY FAIR LADY.** George Bernard Shaw's brilliant romantic play and the internationally acclaimed musical adaptation by Alan Jay Lerner, together in one special edition. (517601—$2.50)

Buy them at your local bookstore or use this convenient coupon for ordering.

NEW AMERICAN LIBRARY,
P.O. Box 999, Bergenfield, New Jersey 07621

Please send me the books I have checked above. I am enclosing $_____
(please add $1.00 to this order to cover postage and handling). Send check or money order—no cash or C.O.D.'s. Prices and numbers are subject to change without notice.

Name _____

Address _____

City _____ State _____ Zip Code _____

Allow 4-6 weeks for delivery.
This offer is subject to withdrawal without notice.